Xyz

Frank Lambert

Cover design by Anton Semenov

Matador
9 Priory Business Park
Kibworth Beauchamp
Leicestershire LE8 0RX, UK
Tel: (+44) 116 279 2299
Fax: (+44) 116 279 2277
Email: books@troubador.co.uk
Web: www.troubador.co.uk/matador

ISBN 978-1784620-127
First Edition, First Print.

British Library Cataloguing in Publication Data.
A catalogue record for this book is available from the British Library.

Typeset in Minion Pro by Troubador Publishing Ltd
Printed and bound in the UK by TJ International, Padstow, Cornwall

Matador is an imprint of Troubador Publishing Ltd

For Mikey Punk

Book two of the *Napoleon Xylophone* trilogy

You begin to see things differently, once you are dead.

Isaac Bonnyman

Scottish Highlands-Lowlands Divide 1888

Isaac Bonnyman had never been this close to a changeling before. He lay perfectly still in the snow, almost not daring to breathe as he stared down the sight of the Springfield Trapdoor rifle. The changeling had gone rogue, they always went that way, it was just a matter of time. How could something capable of morphing into anything it could imagine end up any way other than psychotic? And this particular changeling was psychotic like no other Bonnyman had heard of before. Not only had it killed men, women and children these past three months, it had also eaten them. If Bonnyman's reckoning was correct, its path would bring it back to the place of its first kill.

Over the years, The Cult of the Clan's finest hunters had tried and failed to capture a changeling and Bonnyman was determined he would not make the same mistakes as his peers. Their stories littered the pages of the Cult's history like garbage discarded in the street. He had no intention of laying a trap to ensnare something that could shape-shift itself out of a straight jacket in seconds. No, he wasn't going to capture the changeling; he was going to kill it.

Since reports of the slaughter first spread south, Bonnyman knew it was a changeling responsible for the carnage. What other creature could lay tracks like a mountain lion one step, and a man with feet the size of a giant the next? His studies of changelings had been extensive and, despite their name, he knew they were creatures of habit. That's why he knew the changeling would return to the sight of its first kill. It's morbidly curious nature would eventually get the better of it and draw it here to re-live what had gone before. It was as if there was so much transformation going on in a changeling's life that it had no choice but to seek out the familiarity of past experience. He hoped he hadn't arrived too late and the creature had already returned days ago. He would need a new plan if that was true.

They called this location *Ghalldachd*, the place of the foreigner, and Bonnyman felt every bit the foreigner. It didn't trouble him though, his journeys had taken him far and wide and he was used to being the outsider.

Raising his eyes from the gun sight, he stared across the snow-covered moor. Scotland was bleak at the best of times and in winter, bleakness took on a whole new meaning as the wind and cold sapped everything but the hardiest of spirits. Suddenly feeling tired, he yawned with his eyes closed. When he re-opened them, the changeling stood a few feet in front of him, staring at Bonnyman like he was a meal waiting to be eaten.

The creature had taken on the form of a bear and stood over fifteen feet tall on its hind legs. Its head hadn't morphed into a bear's head, though, instead of a snout, its face was flat and its mouth was twisted, like it had been blown away by a shotgun. The changeling's teeth were the most disturbing part of its appearance. Both top and bottom rows held long, curved incisors, like it had a mouth full of sabre teeth.

Bonnyman's companions reacted quickly. Edwards fired his rifle first, but his aim was wild and inaccurate. Even at this short distance, the bullet only grazed the changeling's shoulder. In response, the changeling roared at Edwards and its arm extended impossibly long as it grabbed hold of him by the hair, pulling him from where he sat prone on the ground. Leaning into the screaming man's neck, it bit his throat away before throwing him back onto the ground.

While the changeling chewed on Edwards' flesh, Bonnyman's other companion, Reed, was more controlled. He carefully aimed his rifle at the creature's chest and slowly pulled the trigger. The changeling was knocked back by the force of the bullet, which hit its chest dead-centre, yet the changeling remained standing as it looked from its chest to Reed.

Reed's hands began to shake as he attempted to load another bullet into his rifle. 'Shoot it,' he yelled at Bonnyman as the bullet slipped from his grasp and he looked up to see the changeling charging at him.

Bonnyman stood up and calmly took aim at the changeling's head, just as it grabbed hold of Reed's arms. However, before he could shoot, the changeling raised one of its legs and pushed it into Reed's chest while yanking on his arms. Bonnyman pulled the trigger and, at the same time, the changeling pulled off both of Reed's arms.

The bullet hit the changeling and half of its head exploded into the air. It turned around and its mouth opened and closed like it wanted to say something, but no sound came from its lips.

Bonnyman dropped his rifle and pulled an axe from his belt. Sprinting towards the changeling, he easily avoided its claws as it awkwardly lunged for him. Ducking below the creature's outstretched arms; he raced behind it where he began to hack at its neck with the axe. The changeling spun around and, this time, a pitiful screech came from its mouth as it attempted to strike Bonnyman with its flailing arms once more. Each time the changeling faced him, Bonnyman side-stepped it, striking from behind with the axe, until the changeling's head flopped to the side, held only by the thinnest tendrils of flesh.

Before Bonnyman could hack off the changeling's head completely, it sank to the floor onto its knees with its head hanging upside down by the side of its arm. It stared at Bonnyman with its one remaining eye and this time when it opened its mouth it did speak.

'My dreams have been haunted by this death for many years,' it said, falling to the floor.

Bonnyman's grip tightened on the shaft of the axe. Incapacitating the changeling had been too easy. It hadn't morphed into something else once. Maybe that's what immortality did to the creatures when they became psychotic; it made them live a death wish at the end. He stared at the changeling's black eye until it lazily drooped shut, then waited a moment before stepping closer to it and raising the axe.

Reed lay on the floor bleeding from the two stubs where his arms had once been connected to his body. 'Isaac,' he pleaded, 'help me.'

Bonnyman stared at Reed, knowing he couldn't help him. He lowered the axe anyway and looked across at his rifle, wondering if he was strong enough to do what he needed to do for his friend.

The changeling opened its eye one last time and stared at Bonnyman. Before he could react, it lunged forward and grabbed hold of his legs and with a scissor-like action; it pressed its arms together until Bonnyman's legs snapped. Bonnyman lost his balance and as he fell forward he raised the axe and swung it one more time, severing the tenuous flesh holding the changeling's head to its body. As he landed on the ground, Bonnyman passed out, knowing the changeling was dead, but knowing also that both of his legs were broken.

***

It was dark when Bonnyman awakened. Pain seared through his whole body and he almost passed out again. He shivered uncontrollably, unsure if the pain was caused by his broken legs or the cold. He knew he couldn't survive out in the open for much longer; he had to get to shelter. He was miles away from the nearest town and by the time he crawled back to the camp they had set up beyond the ridge, he would be dead. He wanted to sleep, he desperately wanted to sleep. However, he knew that if he did, he would never awaken again. He looked around and it appeared as though he was seeing things in black and white due to the way the winter moon illuminated the snow filled landscape. He stared at the changeling's dark bulk and knew what he had to do.

He picked up the axe and started to crawl towards the changeling. As soon as he did the pain intensified. He screamed out loud into the night and when he breathed in the cold air, he felt a new kind of pain inside his throat and chest. Clamping his mouth shut, he breathed heavily through his nose. The pain subsided and he began to crawl again, ignoring the sting in his legs, thinking only about how much he did not want to die. When he reached the changeling, he began to hack at its chest with the axe until an opening appeared. He pulled the skin apart with one hand and the changeling's chest gaped open. He began to pull out its internal organs: the stench was horrific, a testament to death, which served to spur him on in a frenzy. When he had finished, the gaping hole inside the changeling was the size of a man and he slowly crawled into it, closing the wound behind him.

Only then did he allow himself to sleep.

The storm grew worse over the next few days. Bonnyman only opened up the changeling's chest to get snow from outside which he swallowed to ensure he didn't dehydrate. He knew he had to eat, he also knew he could not make it back to the camp and the food stored there. So he slept and tried not to think about food.

It wasn't until the third day that he could no longer resist and started to eat the changeling's semi-frozen flesh from the inside. He ate it for the next two days, washed down with snow, not knowing the consequences to his body that eating changeling flesh would bring. He died four days later. Unaware that he was dead, he continued to eat more of the changeling's flesh.

When he stopped feeling the cold and his broken legs began to repair themselves, he knew something was wrong. The storm had eased and he pulled himself out of the changeling, feeling neither thirsty or cold. He stood up on twisted legs that were no longer broken, but not yet fully healed. By the time he walked back to the camp the overriding feeling he had was one of hunger. Ransacking the store of food at the camp, nothing he ate sated his ever-increasing appetite. In an attempt to take his mind off the intense hunger crippling him, he returned to the changeling kill site, intending to bury his fallen companions, hoping it would take his mind off the hunger.

He found Reed's left arm first, buried beneath the snow near the changeling, and without thinking -without realising- he ate the flesh off the arm in minutes. Reed's right arm was devoured even quicker and when he found the rest of Reed and tasted his brains, the hunger eventually eased and he slept for a day. The hunger returned as soon as he awakened and with it a new kind of intense craving. Desperate, he dug up snow until he found Edwards and ate every scrap of flesh he could remove from his old friend's bones.

Later, when the urge to eat human flesh returned, he knew what he had to do. There was a cabin three miles to the south of the camp. Inside the cabin there were enough humans to keep him fed for a week.

Present Day

Zam stared at the leaves falling from the trees in the field behind the school sports hall. They were mostly coloured green; with the occasional red leaf falling amongst them. He expected to see black leaves too, he wasn't sure why. He stopped thinking about leaves when he heard movement behind. Since Zam returned from the underworld below Newcastle city centre, he had not been bullied by Murgo. It was as if Murgo knew Zam had changed, like his in-built bully sense of when to take advantage of a weaker person and when not to, had warned him of the transformation in Zam's character.

Today was different. Today, Murgo was manic and idiotic, picking on everyone he came across at school. Zam thought he must have been drinking too much Pepsi or eating too many Gum-Gum Beans and he avoided him like he would an uncaged hyena. Things were going fine until break time when Zam went outside and saw the ghost dressed as a butcher cutting ghostly meat with a cleaver. As usual, he watched the ghost out of the corner of his eye. Ghosts seldom talked to Zam. It was only when they realised he could see them that they took an interest in him, which was why Zam always tried to make sure they didn't realise he could see them. He never stared at them outright and acted as if they were not there, no matter how bizarre their behaviour. Even though they didn't speak directly, they communicated in other ways. He could taste the things some ghosts tasted or smell the things they smelled as if he was the ghost. Sometimes, the thoughts they were thinking became his thoughts too, like right now. The butcher ghost wasn't thinking about slicing up a cow or a pig. He was cutting the arm off a man. A man he had killed when he was alive. The same man he had hacked to pieces before discarding his body parts in the sewers.

Murgo spotted Zam behind the sports hall staring out into the fields. Slowly and quietly, he walked up behind him and just as Zam moved to turn around, Murgo grabbed the handles to the wheelchair and jerked it backwards. Zam yelled and the butcher ghost turned around and stared at him. He was now aware that Zam could see him.

'Hey, Cripple,' Murgo said, 'it's been a while since we talked.'

Zam grabbed the wheels and twisted them backwards and forwards, pulling free from Murgo.

Murgo shook his hands. 'Careful, Cripple. That hurt.'

'What do you want?'

'I want to play nark-slap and I know just the cripple to play it with.'

Nark-slap consisted of two people attempting to slap each other's ears whilst avoiding being slapped themselves. It was a painful game, especially the way Murgo played it. Even more so if you were in a wheelchair and it was almost impossible to defend yourself.

'Bog off, Murgo. I'm in no mood for your games.' Zam was pleased to see surprise register on Murgo's face.

'Cripple has found some guts at last.'

Zam felt an uncomfortable tingling sensation against his neck. When he turned around, he saw the butcher ghost had walked over to him. It stood behind him, arcing the cleaver up and down against Zam's neck as if it was attempting to hack off his head. Zam backed away from the ghost, but it followed him, continuing to swing the cleaver against his neck. Each time it did, the cleaver disappeared into Zam's flesh, but it did not cut him, it merely tingled like the icy heat of a low voltage electrical current.

'What's wrong Cripple, your courage left you again?'

Zam tried to ignore the ghost. 'Go away, Murgo.'

Murgo smiled, as if he was about to turn away from Zam; but instead, he turned back into Zam and went to slap him across the ear.

Zam was ready for him and he grabbed hold of

Murgo's hand before he connected with his ear. 'I told you to go away.'

Although his legs were weak, Zam's upper body was muscular from the work it had to do transporting his wheelchair around. Since he had returned from the underworld, he worked out daily with a punch-ball that his grandfather had modified so he could punch it while still in his wheelchair. Zam's upper body reflexes were now sharp and precise.

Murgo wrenched his arm from Zam's grasp. 'Careful, Cripple. There are no teachers around here to help you.'

Zam's disability meant that he could only walk in short spurts with the aid of leg splints and when he did walk, he was unsteady and his movements jerky. For the first time ever, he stood up in front of Murgo, pleased to see he was taller than the bully. He leant into Murgo's face. 'Don't you mean there are no teachers around to help you?'

'Oh yeah, and what are you going to do?' Despite his brave face, Murgo stepped away from Zam.

Zam sat back down in his wheelchair, relieved that he hadn't wobbled or fallen. 'There's a ghost behind me Murgo. It has a butcher's cleaver in its hand. It's trying to cut off my head.'

Murgo sniggered. 'Not only are you a cripple, you are crazy too.'

'Oh yes,' Zam said. 'I'm as crazy as they come.' He turned around and faced the ghost. Feeling its rage and hearing its voice inside its head, he knew exactly what to say to it.

'I hear voices inside my head too,' Zam said to the ghost. He pointed at Murgo. 'He doesn't though. He always makes fun of people who hear voices in their head telling them to kill people. He thinks you are dead. You should probably kill him.'

The butcher ghost stopped hacking Zam and dropped the cleaver to its side. It turned towards Murgo.

Murgo smiled. 'I'm gonna tell everyone you talk to yourself, weirdo.'

Raising the cleaver, the ghost strode towards Murgo and, when it reached him, it hacked at his flesh with the cleaver.

Murgo stopped smiling and his hand darted to wherever the ghostly blade landed on him.

'You can feel it, can't you?' Zam said.

Murgo didn't answer.

Zam did not understand the rules of ghosts. Everyone seemed to be able to see some ghosts. While others, only he and creatures from the underworld saw. 'If you really concentrate,' he said, 'I mean really concentrate. You'll be able to see the ghost trying to cut off your head.'

Murgo backed away from Zam. The ghost followed him, hacking at Murgo as it went. 'It's a trick,' Murgo said, 'you're using a Taser or something.'

'Open your eyes Murgo, you'll see the truth then.'

Murgo continued to pat himself each time the cleaver

was buried in his flesh, all the while his eyes darted from side to side, trying to see how Zam was managing to do whatever it was he was doing.

'It feels like electric ice, doesn't it? Just open your eyes and you can see what's really causing the sensation.'

'Make it stop,' Murgo said, stepping towards Zam and clutching his jacket.

Zam grabbed hold of Murgo's hand and as soon as they touched, Murgo's eyes widened. He stared in the direction of the ghost for a moment and then backed away from Zam.

Even though he no longer touched Zam, Murgo stared like he could still see the butcher ghost. Seeing Murgo's response, the ghost slashed at him with renewed intensity. First his arm, then his chest and then his neck. Murgo stumbled backwards, almost falling to the floor. He started to run. He ran until he disappeared behind the science block, with the ghost running after him, cleaving him like it was never going to stop.

Zam stared in their direction for a long time after they were gone. He knew the underworld experience had changed him. Seeing Murgo run away like a bully showing its true colours with the ghost in pursuit, he wasn't sure if it had been a change for the good or a change for the bad.

Zam slept right through the night for the first time in a long time without being awakened by cramp. And he did not dream about ghosts, or wytes or changelings. He dreamt about flying through a rainforest in an open-cockpit jet fighter, crafted from a liquefied substance that reflected the lush vegetation he flew over.

It felt as if he was flying like the wind.

His leg muscles were tight now, though. It was morning and he lay on his back stretching his right leg as far as it would go, before pulling it back until his heel came as close to the top of his leg as he could manage to take it. He repeated the exercise with his left leg, thinking about Johnny Blunt who also had Hereditary Spastic Paraplegia. Johnny's mother always helped him with his leg exercises and Zam wished he had someone to help him, especially during the night when he was still half asleep. Grandfather was too old to disturb during the night and the one time he did ask for help during the day, it felt like Grandfather was going to break his legs.

After he finished his stretches, he stiffly got out of bed and shuffled into his wheelchair before pushing himself towards the bathroom. His legs seemed to be getting worse and the painkillers were not making much, if any, difference. It was his mental resolution that made the difference. Pain no longer caused him anguish like it used to – it had gone beyond anguish. Pain was like a sixth sense now, one that told him he was still alive.

Zam had prepared the tablets the night before. The yellow one he cut in half, it was supposed to control the spasms. The two white ones he took whole, they were to ease the pain. The blue tablet he only took at night. He never took it last night. It was supposed to help him sleep. There was another tablet, one that was supposed to control his moods. He never, ever took that tablet. He always flushed that tablet down the toilet and the toilet always seemed docile. Thinking about his parents, he swallowed the yellow half-tablet and flushed the white tablets down the toilet.

His parents didn't need him and he didn't need his parents.

It was a school day and, as ever, Zam did not want to go to school. He knew he would not be hassled by Murgo again, not after the incident with the butcher ghost. It wasn't bullying that concerned him about school now. There were only two weeks of term time remaining and he only had one more exam left to do, then school would be finished forever. At least until he started A-levels in September. He wondered if Ezzy would talk to him like she used to, once they started A-levels. He knew she needed time to think after her experience with Mandrake Ackx in the underworld, he just didn't expect it to be so long. He stared at his reflection in the mirror. 'You've lost her Zam,' he said, 'maybe you never had her to begin with.'

Zam had never shaved before. Grandfather had informed him the night before that it was time he started and gave him a steam shaver he had designed and built with Jha Round, his technical assistant. The shaver was the size and shape of a brick and almost too hot to hold in his hand. It hissed like it was angry with Zam; its three rotating shaving heads behind the flimsy looking protective screen looked like they wanted to rip the skin from his face before chewing it up and spitting it back out with a triumphant sizzle. Zam turned the shaver on so that Grandfather would think he was using it, then placed it on the side of the sink and picked up Grandfather's shaving brush. He held the brush under the running tap and lathered it in the Taylor of Old Bond Street shaving soap Grandfather got specially delivered from Selfridges. The sandalwood aroma smelled good as he applied the shaving foam to his face with the brush. Maybe shaving wasn't going to be too bad after all, he thought. Satisfied his face was suitably covered, he picked up Grandfather's wet shaver and carefully scraped the blade across his skin. He stared at his refection in the mirror, almost expecting the skin where he had just shaved to turn red with blood. It didn't and Zam smiled, raising his head, so he could shave his neck.

He paused when he saw the figure standing behind him and quickly turned around. There was no one behind him. He assumed it was just another spirit and turned back towards the mirror. Since he returned from the underworld beneath Newcastle, seeing spirits had become a daily part of his life. Grandfather said it was because he had clairvoyant blood running through his veins and the underworld experience had awakened it. Zam wished he didn't have that kind of blood running inside him almost as much as he wished he didn't have legs that couldn't run.

Gazing into the mirror, he saw the figure standing behind him once more, seemingly staring back at him even though it did not have any eyes. He didn't think it was a spirit. Watching it closely, he saw that it didn't have the same form as the spirits he normally saw. Rather than appearing shade-like, it had more substance, though it was still almost featureless. The more he stared at it, the more it appeared to acquire features. A pair of eyes first, then a nose, then a mouth, until Zam's own reflection and the figure standing in the mirror were identical. As Zam continued to stare, the figure reached forward and a pure white hand came through the mirror. It grabbed hold of Zam by the throat and started to pull him. Instinctively, he jerked backwards, momentarily halting the force tugging him forwards. It didn't last though, and when his twin started to pull harder on his throat, Zam was once more thrust towards the mirror. Just before impact, Zam clamped his eyes shut, expecting his face to smack against solid glass. Instead of bouncing off the hard surface of the mirror, Zam felt suction, like he was being pulled into a liquid vacuum. He opened his eyes and it was like seeing things through water, water he could breathe in. He raised his hands and placed them against the mirror, hoping to push himself out of it but, like his head, his hands encountered no resistance when they touched the mirror and they too entered the world of glass like it was a perfectly natural thing to do. He stared at his twin and it smiled back at him in a way that Zam had never smiled before in his life. Panicking, he grabbed hold of the creature's hand attempting to wrench it from his neck, but it was too strong. The creature stopped drawing Zam into its space, as if it was taunting him and for a split second, it gave him time to think.

Zam remembered the steam shaver and pulled his arm out of the mirror, desperately scrabbling around, searching for it on the sink top. When his fingers touched the hot casing, he quickly grasped hold and pulled it towards the mirror. Before it reached the mirror, he flicked his wrist and the shaver's head hit the tiles above the sink, knocking the flimsy protective screen off. Zam could barely think straight as the creature once more started to pull him further into the mirror until they were nose-to-nose. It stared at him with eyes that seemed confident of what was going to happen next and when Zam finally touched the creature's nose with the tip of his own, he began to disappear. First his nose, then his top lip, then his mouth – as if the creature was absorbing whichever part of Zam's body touched its own.

An eye for an eye, a tooth for a tooth.

Zam's face started to feel numb, like it did when the dentist injected him that day he needed a tooth repairing after Murgo had thrown a cricket ball at him. He couldn't breathe, he couldn't scream and he was sure that in a moment he would no longer be able to think. He still had his arm though and he still held onto the steam shaver and deep inside his mind, he still had the will to fight. *Xyz* – he silently repeated to himself. Those three letters were his mantra whenever he felt under any kind of pressure. Speaking them out loud or silently to himself always gave him an edge. He didn't know why.

Xyz, Xyz, Xyz…

He brought the shaver up like a professional boxer would an uppercut and punched the three rotating shaving heads into the creature's neck, just before Zam's neck began to morph into the creature's neck.

The creature didn't scream, not until it pushed Zam away and its mouth reappeared. Then it screamed like a wild fox in the night.

Zam didn't pull away from the creature, instead, he pressed harder on the shaver, twisting it deeper into its neck. A sound that may have been a growl escaped the creature's lips as it stopped screaming and grabbed hold of his wrist, pulling the shaver away from its neck. With its free hand, it then swiped the side of Zam's head, before it backed away from him, clasping its wound. Despite its efforts to stem the flow of blood, it continued to ooze through its fingers and when it looked up at Zam, both its hatred and its frustration were palpable.

Without waiting for it to recover, Zam pulled his head out of the mirror and wheeled himself away from it. He stared at the creature from a distance, while continuing to hold onto the still rotating shaver in case it was needed again. The creature returned to an indistinct, featureless being, the same as it had been the first time he saw it.

'You got lucky,' its cold voice echoed around the bathroom, 'don't expect to get lucky next time.'

Zam watched as the creature began to fade like mist burnt away by the sun, until it disappeared altogether and all that remained was his own reflection in the mirror. He wondered if he was still sleeping, wondered if his nightmares were seeping into his waking moments. Maybe he was just going crazy. The only sign he was not going crazy was the fine line of blood that slowly trailed down the inside of the mirror. When it reached the mirror's edge, it began to drip and the synchronous echo of each drop of blood that hit the white, porcelain sink below almost felt relaxing.

Zam wiped the remaining shaving cream off his face with a towel and quickly wheeled himself into the main living space of the apartment where his grandfather sat drinking early morning Oolong tea. It wasn't really an apartment; it was the top floor above a bank on Grey Street in Newcastle city centre. The rooms on the floor had been knocked into a single space big enough to house a dozen apartments. Zam's grandfather, Eli Xylophone, owned the bank and the adjoining buildings. He was obsessed with steam technology and everything in the apartment was powered by a steam generator housed in the basement. Despite the vast space, it didn't seem roomy inside as every inch of the area was taken up with Bohemian furniture or partly constructed inventions his grandfather had worked on over the years and haphazardly stored in the apartment. Body parts of mechanical automaton sat on top of a prototype model of a steam airship, an old-style, red telephone kiosk housed a collection of clockwork spiders, while a Norton Commander motorbike with an upgraded, steam propulsion drive was parked next to a Gatling gun modified to fire explosive bullets.

Zam thought his grandfather had made his wealth through banking and selling his inventions, but since he discovered his grandfather's connection with the supernatural underworld beneath Newcastle, he wasn't so sure anymore. What he did know was that most of his inventions not only included 21st century technology, they also included underworld technology.

Zam wheeled himself in front of his grandfather and quickly, and breathlessly, told him about the creature pulling him inside the mirror and how he managed to escape using the steam shaver his grandfather had made for him. When he finished he only had one question: 'What was it that attacked me?'

Eli got up from the curvaceous chair he had been sitting in whilst listening to Zam talk and leaned down, gently lifting Zam's chin, examining his bruised neck. 'We need to get you to a doctor,' he said.

'I don't need any more tablets.'

Eli squinted and pulled the neck of Zam's t-shirt further open, revealing red lines of swelling on the back of his neck and shoulders. 'Did the creature give you these welts too?'

'No, that was a butcher ghost at school yesterday.'

Eli frowned, ready to ask another question, but Zam beat him to it.

'Tell me what attacked me in the mirror, Grandfather?'

Taking his hand away from Zam's t-shirt, Eli sat down again. 'I can guess what it was, Napoleon, but I do not know for certain.'

Now it was Zam's turn to frown, as he considered asking Grandfather not to call him Napoleon for the gazillionth time. For the gazillionth time, he decided against it.

'What do you think it was then?'

'I think it was a doppelganger.'

'Huh?'

'A doppelganger. It's a creature that takes on the identity of whoever it manages to absorb.'

'That's exactly how it felt, like it was trying to absorb me…. Why would it want to be me, though?'

'I do not know. We need Hestia to answer that particular question.' Eli watched as Zam shook his head from side-to-side and waited a moment before speaking again. 'I'm afraid you have no say in this, Napoleon. Your life is at risk. I won't allow anything to happen to you. We need Hestia's help.'

'Stop calling me Napoleon. I hate that name,' Zam said.

'Your grandmother chose your name. It has a special meaning for her.'

Zam squeezed his hands tightly together. 'I'm sorry. I don't hate it really. I just prefer being called Zam. You never talk about Grandmother anyway.'

'No,' Eli said and from his tone, Zam knew he would say no more about her today.

'Isn't there anyone else we can ask for help other than Hestia?'

'Hestia is not so bad.'

'She killed Rat, remember?'

Rat was Zam's polecat. He attacked Hestia when it looked like Hestia was going to attack Zam. The more he thought back to that day, the more confusing things became. He wasn't even sure if Hestia would have attacked him if Rat had not stopped her, or if she would have merely stopped Zam from zapping her father with the laser he was about to fire at him.

'Rat was attempting to pull her ear off at the time, if I remember correctly,' Eli said.

'She didn't have to kill him.'

'Hestia has been more than a friend to us.'

'I know, it's just… I don't know.'

Eli scratched his chin. 'Come with me,' he said, heading for the door at the far end of the apartment, 'it's time I showed you something important.'

Zam followed close behind in his wheelchair, hoping Grandfather was ready to show him something more interesting than important. The door led into the adjoining building. Again, the space had been knocked into one vast area, but instead of housing an apartment, this space housed a workshop. Jha Round stood at a desk in the centre of the workshop eating a doughnut and drinking coffee while staring at a computer screen which was running numbers up and down the display. He was dressed in his usual jeans and sweatshirt and he wore circular, steel-rimmed glasses, even though he had perfect eyesight. *'They make me look like John Lennon,'* he told Zam when he asked Jha why he was wearing glasses with clear lenses. Zam thought he looked like John Lennon even without the glasses. It was just a shame he didn't sound like Lennon when he sang, instead of sounding like a seized wheel bearing.

Jha turned around to face them as they entered and smiled lopsidedly.

'Have you been up all night again?' Eli asked when they reached him.

'Sleep is for those who only want to live half a life,' Jha said in his Polish accent, 'I want to live a full life where sleep only plays a supporting role, not the main event.'

Eli placed his hand on Jha's shoulder. 'I want to download the dongulator into the wheelchair.'

'You're going to bring Q back?' Zam said, excitedly.

'I had planned on completing some more testing before I introduced you to Q again, Napoleon, but I think it's only right that you should be present when Q is re-born.'

'My new wheelchair is finally ready to download Q's memory banks into?'

Eli smiled. 'Yes, the wheelchair, at least, is ready.' He nodded to Jha and his technical assistant began to type into the keyboard. When he stopped typing, Zam heard the whirr of motors as the floor to his right opened up into a circular hole and a platform began to slowly rise. When it was fully elevated, Zam stared at the wheelchair positioned in the centre of the platform for the first time. He was disappointed.

'That's the new Q?' he said.

The wheelchair was minimally constructed with a matt black, tubular sub frame and silver fastenings. It had two rugged looking rear wheels and two smaller front wheels. A leather seat that wouldn't look out of place in a sports car sat between two chunky armrests and Zam guessed that the black box beneath the seat housed the power and drive units. Zam thought the wheelchair looked cool, but it was smaller than the original Q and he doubted it had as many features.

He doubted it could fly.

'It's not Q yet,' Eli said, as he walked across to the wheelchair, 'it hasn't got his brain.' Taking a remote from his pocket, he pressed a button and the wheelchair bleeped once before a small cover on the right hand side armrest slid open to reveal what looked like some form of electronic connection point. Eli's hand disappeared inside his pocket once more and this time he pulled out the dongulator. Zam recognised it as the one his grandfather had used to download Q's memory banks onto only seconds before he was destroyed by Mandrake Ackx. Eli placed the dongulator into the armrest and slid the cover closed. He pressed another button on the remote and this time the wheelchair bleeped twice.

'Q, can you hear me?' Eli said, after a short while.

There was no reply.

'Maybe we need to run a disc scan,' Jha said.

Zam wheeled closer to the platform. 'What's wrong, Grandfather? Is the dongulator broken?'

The wheelchair suddenly jerked forwards on the platform, then backwards. Then it remained still. 'Zam,' it said, in an unfamiliar voice, 'everything is turning black.'

'Q, is that you?'

'I feel different, Zam.'

'Do you remember what happened in the underworld?'

'I remember Mandrake Ackx, and then darkness. I remember...Did I die? Am I dead, Zam? Are you dead too?'

'No, we aren't dead, Q.'

'I see you Zam, you haven't changed. But I have, I don't recognise me at all.'

Zam glanced at his grandfather and then back at Q 'When Ackx touched you, the wheelchair you were loaded onto, it… it kinda shattered into pieces. It's gone. Grandfather downloaded your memory banks into a new wheelchair. You look really cool.'

'Why didn't I turn into a ghost when I died? I always wanted to be a ghost.'

'You didn't die, Q. You've just been... sleeping.'

'I always dream when I sleep. You know that. And I haven't been dreaming this time. If I wasn't dreaming, I can't have been sleeping. I must have been dead.'

Zam stared at his grandfather, this time not turning away from him.

'Run a function check, Q,' Eli said. 'See if everything is working as it should be.'

'I already have. Everything is functioning perfectly, except for me.'

'What's wrong with you Q?' Eli asked.

'I am not the same.'

'You are the same, Q, it's just the equipment you are attached to that's different.'

'Yes, I can see the wheelchair is different, but so am I.'

'How are you different, Q?'

'It feels like I am dead. It feels like I should not be here. You should not have brought me back to life.'

'Would you do me a favour, Q?' Eli said.

'What do you want me to do?'

'Would you let Zam take you out for a test ride?'

'I, I…'

'Zam needs you.'

Q slowly wheeled back and forth. 'Zam. Where is Rat?' he asked.

Zam flinched, he always felt emotional whenever he thought about his polecat. 'He's dead. Hestia killed him.'

'Can't you bring him back to life, like you did me?'

'Q…' Eli began.

29

'We can't do that, Q,' Zam said, interrupting his grandfather, 'we didn't download his memories before he died, like we did yours.'

'You mean you could not download a living creature's memories, like you could mine,' Q said. 'I guess I have never been alive.'

'Q...' Zam started.

Q cut him off. 'What about Ezzy, is she dead? And where is Slink?'

Zam lowered his eyes; he always did that whenever he thought about Ezzy these days. 'Ezzy is fine. She is with her mother. Slink, isn't a ghost anymore. He faded away after we defeated Ackx.'

It was a moment before Q responded. 'Faded away to where?'

'To wherever ghosts go when they no longer need to haunt our world.'

'I found this voice in my database.' Q said in the voice of Clint Eastwood. 'I like the sound of this voice.'

'I always liked Clint's voice on you,' Zam said. 'It makes you sound ultra-cool.'

'I guess I am ultra-cool, Zam. Even if I'm not really alive. Hey, what do you say we go take these wheels out and see how they roll?'

Zam smiled. 'I say that's a great idea, Q.'

Q wheeled himself off the platform and stopped beside Zam. 'Shuffle across into my seat and let me show you how a real wheelchair feels.'

Zam laughed. 'Sure thing, Q. It's great having you back.'

'It's great to see you alive and well too, Zam.'

Zam got into Q and patted the armrests. 'I'll go get ready for school. We can try you out on the way.'

'There is no school today, Zam,' Eli said. 'I want to keep you close at hand, until we know what we are dealing with here.'

Zam was pleased about school, but not so pleased about being kept close to Grandfather's side.

'I can look after myself.'

'I'm sure you can. This is not about you looking after yourself, it is about me knowing where you are and that you are safe.'

'When will we know what we are dealing with?'

'After we have talked to Hestia. Hopefully, she will be here later today.'

'You've contacted her already? How did you do that?'

Eli looked over the top of his glasses at Zam, as if he was unsure how to respond. 'She always knows when I worry about you. She always comes to see me then.'

'How could she know that?'

'It's just the way it is.'

'Grandfather, are you a supernatural creature? Are you a changeling too?'

'No. I'm not a changeling,' Eli scratched his chin. 'In some ways, we are all supernatural. Both human and supernatural creatures are connected. We breathe the same air and our minds process the same things.'

'That doesn't explain how Hestia would know you are concerned about me? Has she put you under some kind of spell?'

'The time I spent in the underworld with Ackx and Hestia changed things inside of me. I was exposed to the supernatural for such a long time that I am marked. If I so choose I can share my emotions, the way I feel, with certain supernatural beings.'

'You mean you are telepathic?'

'In a way, it is a form of telepathy. More so, it is a kind of shared perception. I cannot speak to Hestia, I can only share emotion.'

'Can you share the same things with me?'

'Up until your clairvoyant side first revealed itself in the underworld, I did not think so.'

'And now?'

Before Eli could answer, a jet-black crow with brown eyes flew through the open doorway and glided into the workshop. It landed next to Eli and immediately began to preen its wing feathers. A moment later it started to unfurl, like a flag in a gust of wind. When it had finished morphing, a woman stood next to Eli. She was unclothed, but her long black hair – so long it touched the floor, covered most of her body. Her brown eyes glistened as they stared at Zam.

Zam had never seen Hestia in this form before, he was used to seeing her in the form of a little girl, a sabre-toothed alabaster tiger, or a giant polecat.

'Hestia,' Eli said, 'thank you for coming so quickly.'

Jha backed away from the computer he was standing next to, until he came to a halt against a large electrical panel. 'Is there something I need to know, Eli?'

Eli smiled. 'There is nothing to worry about, Jha. Hestia is a friend. She is also a changeling.'

Jha looked slightly less anxious. 'Oh, in that case, I guess there is nothing to worry about...'

'Changelings, ghosts and doppelgangers are part of everyday life, now that you work for Grandfather,' Zam said, as he started to wheel Q towards the exit. 'I'm going to test out Q, see you later.'

'I see Napoleon has still not forgiven me,' Hestia said in a melodic, child-like voice.

Zam loved hearing Hestia speak; her voice had the same effect upon him as his favourite music. He hated liking anything about her,

'You killed Rat. That's all I think about when I see you.'

'You have a magical voice,' Jha said to Hestia, 'have you ever considered singing in a band?'

'We haven't got time for this,' Eli said. 'Napoleon, you need to stay here, Q's testing can be completed later.' He turned away from Zam without giving him the opportunity to respond. 'How is your father, Hestia?'

Hestia turned towards Eli. 'He is old,' was all she said by way of explanation. 'What is troubling you?'

Eli looked disappointed at her bluntness. 'I think a

doppelganger is hunting Napoleon,' he said, before proceeding to explain what had happened earlier that morning.

Hestia remained silent as he talked. When he finished, she ran her fingers through her hair. 'It is not surprising Napoleon should be hunted in this way. After he defeated my father he became valued to certain creatures of the underworld.'

'I was afraid that would happen,' Eli said. 'How do we call them off?'

'I have already called them off. At least, I have called off the Angles.'

Eli looked surprised. 'You lead the Angles now?'

'Yes, since my father's demise, it has fallen on me to lead.'

'You never wanted to lead.'

'There are many things I would have chosen not to do, if the choice were mine to make.' Hestia turned towards Zam. 'Tell me more about this doppelganger, what did it say to you when it pulled you into the mirror?'

Zam looked as if he was going to ignore Hestia. 'It didn't say a word,' he eventually said, 'other than *I got lucky*. It only said that after I chewed it up with Grandfather's shaver.'

Hestia considered Zam's words. 'Most doppelgangers are extremely talkative. They like to unsettle their victims by speaking in exactly the same voice as the person they are about to absorb. This one saying so little says a lot about who it possibly is.'

'You know this doppelganger?' Eli said.

'If it is who I think it is, I know it by reputation only.'

'Who do you think it is?'

'A doppelganger who goes by the name of Krackle.'

'It has a name?' Zam asked.

'Why wouldn't it have a name?' Hestia replied.

'I don't know. I guess I thought it was just like… I don't know.'

'How do we make contact with it?' Eli asked. 'We have to call it off Napoleon.'

'We can't call it off. If it is Krackle, then only Isaac Bonnyman can do that.'

'Who is Isaac Bonnyman?' Zam asked.

'He commands the Picts. Krackle is a Pict,' Hestia said.

'A Pict?'

'Picts are the underworld creatures of Scotland,' Eli said.

Zam frowned. 'So why don't you call them Scottish instead of Picts?'

'Scotland was called Pictland long before it was ever called Scotland. Just like England was known as the Land of Angles.

Zam turned towards Hestia. 'Is Bonnyman a changeling like you?'

'No, he is a zombie,' Hestia said.

Zam smirked. 'Zombies are brainless, how can a zombie command any part of the underworld?'

'Real zombies are not like they are in the movies, Napoleon,' Eli said. 'I've met Isaac, he is intelligent – he is brutal.'

'If he is so intelligent, why would he send a doppelganger to attack me?'

'I don't think he would,' Hestia said, 'it is more likely that Krackle is acting on his own. There is much respect to be had from being the one who defeats Mandrake Ackx's conqueror.'

'How do I kill this Krackle?' Zam asked.

Now it was Hestia's turn to frown. 'You do not kill him. You stay away from mirrors and reflective surfaces until we speak to Isaac.'

'It's a good job you are not Ezzy,' Q said. 'She is attached to reflective surfaces.'

'We need to travel to Edinburgh then,' Eli said.

Hestia nodded. 'Yes, Isaac doesn't stray too far from the underworld beneath Edinburgh.'

'What if you are wrong and he did send the doppelganger after me?' Zam said.

Hestia stared into Zam's eyes. 'Then we are in for an interesting time in Edinburgh. Unlike the creatures you think they are, zombies are actually formidable opponents.'

'Do they still die if you blast their heads off?'

'What is it about you and killing supernatural creatures?' Hestia said.

Zam raised an eyebrow. 'Maybe it has something to do with supernatural beings always trying to kill me.'

'Would someone mind telling me what is going on here?' Jha asked. He was standing by the computer again and seemed to have recovered his composure.

'Do you remember me telling you that working for me would sometimes be quirky when I first offered you the job?' Eli said.

'Yes,' Jha replied, 'you also said it could be rewarding in a curious kind of way.'

'Yes, I said that too. Well, this is the rewarding quirkiness I spoke about. Do you have a problem with it?'

Jha removed his glasses and rubbed his nose on his arm. 'You never mentioned anything about people trying to kill other people.'

'No, I never mentioned that.'

'Is there anything else you never mentioned that you think I need to know?'

'Nothing that immediately springs to mind.'

'What about werewolves?' Zam said.

'And vampires,' Q added.

Jha smiled. 'Vampires and werewolves are cool. As long as there is no one dressed in a gorilla suit. I hate it when I come across someone dressed like that; it gives me the ultra-creeps.'

Eli smiled. 'There are no people like that in my world, Jha.'

'In that case,' Jha put his glasses back on and raised his thumb, 'I'm with you all the way.'

'We should leave right away,' Hestia said, 'there may be more than just a doppelganger hunting Napoleon.'

Zam winced at Hestia's words. He didn't like the idea

of being hunted, yet at the same time he was nervously excited. He remembered how being so close to death in the underworld made him feel more alive. He stared at Hestia, wondering what she really wanted. 'Why are you helping us?' he asked.

Hestia looked from Eli to Zam. 'Anything that keeps me away from my father is a welcome relief. Since you crushed his will, he might as well be dead.'

Zam was disappointed he didn't get the opportunity to test Q when Hestia insisted that they set off for Edinburgh right away. Eli didn't like the idea of Zam missing more school than he had anticipated, but he agreed with Hestia when she asked what was more important: school or Zam losing his life?

'You need some clothes,' Eli said to Hestia as they prepared to leave, 'we can't have you walking around naked like that.'

Hestia looked at Eli like he was dressed in a gorilla suit and immediately morphed into a Rottweiler the size of a lion. 'You still think I should wear clothes,' she challenged Eli.

Eli walked up to Hestia and began to stroke her neck. 'You may act all aggressive, showing off your teeth like that, but underneath I know you are all gums and gentleness.'

Hestia started to growl, guttural and aggressive. 'You

don't know me at all,' she said, before morphing back into the woman she had been earlier.

Zam turned his back on Grandfather and Hestia, not sure why he didn't like to see them acting that way. He headed for his room, where he dressed and prepared for the journey to Edinburgh. When he was finished, he entered the main living area and wondered where Hestia had got the clothes she was wearing as she exited the guest room dressed in a black polo neck jumper and beige trousers.

'Maybe you should tie your hair up,' Eli said when he saw her.

Hestia's hair still touched the floor. She smiled at Eli as it began to shrink until it just touched her shoulders. 'Anything else you don't like about me?' she asked.

'You look… perfect,' Eli replied.

Zam thought he saw Grandfather blush. He had never seen him blush in all the time he had lived with him.

'I think Eli has the hots for Hestia,' Q whispered to Zam.

Zam frowned. 'Don't be stupid, Grandfather is far too old, and besides, Hestia is a changeling.'

'Yeah, you are probably right,' Q said.

Eli had converted the service lift so that it opened up directly into the apartment to give better access for Zam. It was spacious enough so that Zam didn't feel claustrophobic inside like he did in most lifts. The lift creaked into life and when the door opened a moment later, Jha stood there, smiling like someone who was struggling to smile for a photograph they didn't want taken.

'Everything is ready,' he said. 'Er, I was thinking, do I need a cross or silver bullets, maybe a rabbit's foot for good luck?'

'We make our own luck,' Hestia said. 'Perhaps some holy water would prove useful, though.'

'Holy water, really?' Jha said.

Hestia shook her head from side to side and headed for the lift without responding.

Zam smiled despite not wanting to.

Eli looked troubled and walked over to Zam, placing his hand on his shoulder. 'I am sorry for putting you in danger again,' he said.

'This isn't your fault,' Zam said, looking up at his grandfather.

Eli squeezed Zam's shoulder. 'I'm afraid it is.'

'How is it your fault?'

'I should never have got involved with your grandmother.'

'You never talk about her.'

'No. But I will, once this is finished. I'll tell you everything then.'

'Why can't you tell me now?'

'Now is not the time. It will only distract you when you need to remain focused on the doppelganger.'

Zam bit his lip. 'Are you okay, Grandfather?'

'I'm fine,' Eli said, grabbing hold of Q and pushing him into the lift.

'Is Grandmother still alive?' Zam asked as the lift began its descent.

'Yes,' Eli said.

Hestia turned towards Eli as he spoke and looked as though she too would speak, but she remained silent.

'When the time is right, I'd like to know everything about her,' Zam said.

The lift came to a halt at ground level and Jha pulled the concertina doors open.

'When the time is right,' Eli said, 'do not judge her too harshly. Remember that some decisions are made through necessity rather than personal choice.'

They exited the lift and walked along the white walled corridor towards a door at the far end.

'There you go again, sounding just like Hestia,' Zam said.

'What do you mean?' Eli asked, as they reached the door and he pressed his finger against a recognition unit mounted on the wall. The unit bleeped once and then the door swung open.

'Hestia always talks about choices sometimes not being choices. She believes in fate.'

They stepped out into Grey Street and Zam saw that the day was overcast with a slight breeze. Since he had been in the underworld and experienced life underneath the shifting red clouds there, Zam no longer complained about the ubiquitous grey clouds that covered north-east England. These days he had started to appreciate the wind, the rain and the cold.

'I believe that choices are an illusion,' Hestia said.

The Mercedes was just ahead, in Grandfather's private parking bay at the side of the building. They made their way towards it with Jha leading them.

Zam turned to face Hestia. 'If we never have a choice in life, and everything is predefined, what's the point of living?'

'I didn't say we never have a choice, we do. I said that choices are an illusion. We make our decisions based on the choices given to us, but our decisions are set before we even make them. We are already the choices we make from the very first day we are born.'

'That's the same thing, said in a different way. You are saying we can't make a choice, so what is the point of living a life like that?'

'The point of living life is to dream,' Q said.

'You will dream again,' Zam said to Q. 'I'm sure of it.'

'I'm sure too,' Q replied. 'What troubles me is why I didn't dream when I was stored in the dongulator.'

Zam didn't know how to respond to Q, so he remained silent and hoped Q would eventually forget about his time in limbo, when he was nothing more than an unused program. He knew Q would never forget, just like he knew Q was more than a computer program stored on a memory chip.

At the parking bay they entered the extra-long Mercedes-Benz Viano that Eli had converted to make transporting wheelchairs easier. Jha sat in the driver's seat, while Eli sat next to him in the front passenger seat. Zam and Hestia settled in the rear, with an empty seat between them. The Mercedes was big enough so that Q could fit in the back along with all of the luggage and Jha's tools, which he took everywhere with him. It wasn't until an hour or so later, when they reached Berwick and Zam started to daydream about flying beneath blood red skies that he saw Krackle in the rear view mirror. The doppelganger was in the form of the non-descript shadow that Zam had first seen in the bathroom mirror. It quickly began to morph into a duplicate of Zam. Smiling at him, Krackle pointed his finger at Zam and then pointed it at itself.

Zam pinched his nose and raised his head, pretending to shave with an invisible shaver. When he reached his neck, he began to choke as if he was being chewed up by Grandfather's steam shaver.

Krackle stopped smiling.

'What are you doing?' Hestia said.

'The doppelganger is in the rear view mirror,' Zam replied.

Hestia looked up at the mirror, but when she did, Krackle dissolved into glass before she saw him.

'Do not treat a doppelganger as though it is not a threat,' she said to Zam.

'I'm not,' Zam replied. 'I'm treating it as though it's a threat that I can have some fun with. There isn't enough fun in my life right now so I have to grab it with both hands whenever it presents itself.'

Hestia turned away from Zam, smiling to herself. 'Your grandfather said you have started to see ghosts since you were in the underworld.'

'Yes.'

'Do they harm you?'

'Some try to.'

'We need to stop that happening.'

'How do we do that?'

'I can show you.'

'Do you see ghosts too?'

'Yes.'

'What about the butcher?'

'The butcher?'

'Yes, the butcher ghost sitting next to you.'

Hestia turned to the empty seat between them.

Zam sighed. 'You can't see him can you?'

'No.'

'Why not? You are a supernatural.'

'Some ghosts prefer to remain hidden.'

'Ghosts can choose who can see them and who can't?'

'Some can, not all.'

'This ghost has been following me since yesterday. None have ever done that before. Oh, and it's a psychopath.'

'Psychopaths get to be ghosts too, but wheelchairs don't!' Q said from the rear of the Mercedes. 'Where is the fairness in that?'

Zam turned towards Q and shrugged his shoulders.

'It follows you because it sees something in you that it wants or needs,' Hestia said.

'Like what?' Zam asked.

'Usually, it is energy that a ghost desires the most.'

'What kind of energy?'

'The energy inside all of us. The energy of life.'

'Life, what does that look like?'

Hestia thought for a moment before speaking. 'To a ghost, it is like an aura. Like you are inside an aura of coloured light.'

'Why would a ghost be attracted to my aura?'

'Because you are alive and it is dead. Dead and lost.'

'Sometimes I feel dead and lost too.'

'I am sorry.'

'No need, it's not your fault.'

'I wish I had done more to help you.'

'Would you have killed me in the underworld, when I was about to attack your father and you killed Rat?'

Hestia looked troubled. 'I truly do not know. I was only thinking about stopping you from harming my father. Above all else, parents mean everything to supernatural creatures. Even at the expense of their own children.'

'That's dumb.'

'In one sense, yes.'

'In every sense.'

'I can't see your butcher ghost, Zam,' Q said. 'Does he hurt you?'

'No he doesn't, not since yesterday.'

'What does it want?'

'It wants to kill everyone.'

'Even you, Zam?'

'I don't think so, not anymore.'

'You must command it to leave you,' Hestia said.

'I've already tried to do that. It doesn't seem to hear what I am saying, like it is blanking me out in some way.'

Hestia placed her hand on the seat where the ghost sat, as if she was attempting to feel its presence. 'This is unusual.'

The ghost turned towards Hestia and tried to hack off her head with its ghostly cleaver.

'Can you feel that?' Zam asked.

'Yes,' Hestia said.

'You'll have welts in the morning on your neck.'

'I don't do welts, I'm a changeling,' Hestia said. 'Touch the ghost,' she continued, 'and use your mind to imagine your hand is a ghost hand, so that it really can touch the ghost. Then command it to leave.'

Zam hesitated, then moved his hand towards the ghost and went to grab it by its wrist, imagining that his hand was a ghost hand like Hestia had instructed him to do. At first he couldn't feel anything, then his fingers began to tingle, then the ghost turned to face him and Zam felt like he was indeed holding its wrist. 'I command you to leave this car,' he said.

The ghost narrowed its eyes, but did not move.

'I command you to leave,' Zam repeated.

The ghost continued to ignore him. Then, it began to chop at his neck with the cleaver.

'It didn't work,' Zam said.

'I can't feel it anymore,' Hestia replied.

'That's because it's trying to chop off my head instead of yours now.'

'Oh,' Hestia said.

'Is there nothing you can do to help him?' Eli said, with a pained expression on his face.

'Not just yet.'

'It's okay, Grandfather. I'm starting to get used to this kind of thing.'

Eli frowned. 'I do not want you becoming accustomed to this kind of thing.'

'Isaac might be able to help,' Hestia said.

'How can he help?' Zam asked. 'Do you think my ghost is a Pict too?'

Hestia shook her head from side to side. 'No, I don't. Isaac is a zombie, he is dead. He should be able to communicate with the ghost at the very least.'

'What do we do in the meantime?' Q asked. 'Zam can't have a ghost trying to chop his head off until we talk to Bonnyman.'

Hestia moved her hand towards the ghost again. 'I command you to leave the boy alone,' she said.

The ghost ignored her.

'It's okay Hestia,' Zam said, 'it only tingles my skin.

Jha, can you play some music, it'll take my mind off the psychopath sitting next to me.'

'Sure,' Jha said. 'What would you like to listen to?'

'*Broken Bells* would be good.'

Jha switched the music system on and then selected a track. *Broken Bells* started to sing about dreams in October.

Zam closed his eyes, focusing on the music and the tingling sensation the cleaver made against his skin. He thought about Ezzy, how she would never be his girlfriend and he wondered where his mother and father were. He suddenly felt grateful to the ghost and the distraction the tingling made to the pain in his legs. If the ghost could somehow cut his legs off and take the pain away for good, he thought that maybe it would be for the best. If the choice were his to make, he knew he would choose to keep his legs attached to his body. Just like the decisions he made shaped him, he also knew that his legs were part of who he was too.

6

Zam awakened to the sound of Grandfather and Jha arguing over who should take the luggage inside the house. In the end, they both carried it inside. Grandfather had arranged for them to stay at a friend's holiday home, which was currently unoccupied. The property was a substantial, four-storey Georgian townhouse, located on Walker Street in the centre of Edinburgh. After he had finished unloading the luggage, Jha opened the boot and got Q out, placing him next to the passenger door for Zam. Before Zam exited the Mercedes, he stared at the butcher ghost which appeared to be sleeping. Zam was surprised, he didn't think ghosts slept. Opening the car door as quietly as he could, he carefully slipped out and shuffled into Q's seat.

The butcher ghost immediately awakened, passed through the car door without opening it, and moved as though he was going to strike Zam with the cleaver. Standing next to Zam with the meat cleaver raised, it remained immobile as it stared at the house next door to the one they were staying in, as if there was something of great importance to look at.

Zam saw nothing remarkable as he stared at the house. The only difference was some scaffolding erected on the front of the house. Zam couldn't think why scaffolding would be of interest to the ghost.

'My sensors can see your ghost,' Q said, as Zam buckled himself into his seat. 'I wonder why he's decided to reveal himself to me now?'

'Well, you haven't got a head,' Zam said, 'it can't be that he wants to chop it off.'

'Maybe it's my wheels he's after?'

'What would he want with your wheels?'

'I don't know. What would he want with your head?'

'Maybe he just gets a buzz from chopping things up.'

Q turned towards the ghost. 'He looks kinda sad, like a little boy who has lost his mother.'

'I was thinking more like someone who has lost his collection of severed heads.'

The ghost suddenly growled like a guard dog spotting an intruder.

Q coughed. 'Maybe we should stop talking about him.'

'I'm with you on that,' Zam said, as he wheeled himself towards the gate leading to the house. Before he got there, he stopped when he saw something move on the paving. He must have been mistaken, he thought, it can't have been moving. It was a finger. Not a human finger, more like one of those synthetic Halloween joke fingers that belong to a haggard witch. He bent down and picked it up. It felt too heavy to be synthetic, too much like flesh to be a joke. Studying it carefully, he saw the bone at the stump where it had been cut from a hand was yellow and the streaks of blood were more black than red. He looked around, as if he was going to see the owner of the finger step up to him and ask for it back.

The finger owner wasn't anywhere to be seen. Instead, he noticed a girl at the end of the street staring at him. She was Zam's age, maybe slightly younger and she started to walk towards him, falteringly, like she knew Zam, but wasn't sure if it was really him. He liked the way she moved, more than that, he liked the way she looked. Her black, shoulder length hair was striking, with a perfectly straight fringe cut just above her eyebrows and skin so white it made her hair appear all the more black. He was about to wheel himself towards her but stopped when he heard the crash and saw the bowling ball shoot out of the side of the scaffolding. He knew it was going to hit the girl, yet he couldn't do anything about it other than stare as sadness and regret filled his mind like he had just found and lost a soul mate.

The wraith unzipped the bag covering the bowling ball and stepped out of the bedroom window onto the scaffolding that had been erected by the roofing contractor replacing tiles. It stared down at the boy below, watching as he stretched his arms and yawned. He was wearing black jeans and a black t-shirt with some pattern on it the wraith didn't recognise. Half of his hair was coloured black, while the other half was dark blue. The boy suddenly began to talk to himself and he was smiling. It seemed that the one who vanquished Mandrake Ackx was psychotic, how perfectly understandable.

The wraith had originally planned to simply launch the bowling ball over the edge of the scaffolding rail, knowing her superior throwing skills would result in a strike, but she had become bored waiting for him to arrive. While she waited, the wraith erected an intricate path for the ball to follow, using building materials and furnishings she had found in the bedroom. She bit off one of her own fingers and placed it on the ground near the entrance to the house where the boy was staying, certain his curious mind would not be able to ignore it. The wraith was able to control who saw the finger and who did not see it by simply thinking it visible or invisible. She could keep the boy fixed in the target zone investigating the finger while the bowling ball took its intricately slow path towards him. As for her finger, she would pick it up later and get a Wiccan to sew it back on for the price of a bowl of soup.

The plan was working like a perfect nightmare. The boy had the finger in his hand now, studying it like it was an important puzzle to decipher. The wraith carefully aligned the boy up with her thumb and when she was happy that he was in exactly the right position, she set the bowling ball rolling on its way down the metal guttering she had carefully positioned along the length of boarding. At the end of the guttering, the ball landed in a cupboard drawer which immediately tilted backwards flipping the ball into a hole in the scaffolding. The ball fell through the hole onto the level below and landed on a rug suspended between a window ledge and the scaffold rail. It rolled down the carpet, rapidly picking up speed and if the carpet hadn't pulled away from the window ledge, it would have continued over the edge of the scaffold on a perfect trajectory towards the boy. But the carpet did pull away from the ledge, because the wraith may have been good at throwing, but she was hopeless at nailing things down. Instead of flying towards the boy, it landed on the wooden scaffold boards with a thud before it hit the wall and bounced from side to side between the wall and the kick boards, almost coming to a stop at the far end of the scaffolding. It didn't stop because the scaffold boards had not been installed level, so it slowly began to roll in the opposite direction from where it had originally travelled, taking it further away from the boy. By the time it reached the other end of the scaffold it was travelling fast enough to bump itself onto a length of guttering the wraith had discarded earlier. The guttering was balanced on the end kick board and when the ball crossed its centre of balance the guttering tipped and the ball flew over the edge, dropping off the scaffold.

'Oops,' the wraith said, before disappearing back through the window into the bedroom. She walked past the two contractors lying face down on the floor, who she had slain earlier and headed for the stairway, still unsure whether to face the wrath of the bandaged man or to disappear for a few years until the corpse dust settled.

In the end, she decided to see if there was any more fun to be had in the house.

As Zam looked up, he saw the bowling ball drop from the scaffold. He also saw a figure looking down at him. Although it was human in shape, it was obviously not human in any other way. It was formed of different shades of grey and every part of it seemed to move, like a silk cloth in the breeze. Its long, streaked hair hung loose and covered most of the creature's face, leaving just its eyes visible. They were the only part of the creature that wasn't grey. Even at this distance he could see they were black and intense. It held onto the scaffold as if the scaffold would fall down if it let go.

As the bowling ball flew from the end of the framework, Zam knew exactly where it was going to land, but he was frozen, unable to shout even a warning. The ball hit the girl on her forehead, just as she looked up to see where Zam was staring. She fell to the ground instantly, while the bowling ball rolled into the gutter and came to a stop next to a car tyre. Zam hurriedly wheeled towards the girl with images of the first aid course he had attended at school sweeping through his mind. When he reached her, he knew none of the techniques he had learned during the course would help. The girl's spirit stood next to her body, staring down at it with a mix of curiosity and horror.

'I'm dead,' the spirit girl said with a slight Scottish accent, 'I'm actually dead.'

'It's okay,' Zam said.

The spirit girl turned towards him. 'How can it be okay? Look at me. I'm… a ghost.'

A young boy on a battered BMX turned the corner into the street where Zam and the spirit girl stood. He was riding on the pavement, going too fast. He swerved to avoid Zam and passed straight through the spirit girl without even knowing he had.

'Sorry, Wheelchair Boy,' he shouted at Zam as he continued to speed away.

'I'm a ghost,' the spirit girl repeated. She stared at Zam. 'He didn't see me. How can you see me?'

'It's a long story, something to do with clairvoyant blood running through my veins. I think I got it from my grandmother.'

The spirit girl wept. 'There is so much I wanted to do.'

'You still can. You are going to a better place.'

'What do you mean?'

Zam wondered what he meant too. 'Err, you are going

57

to Heaven, so there will be loads of… stuff you can do there.'

'How do I get to Heaven?'

Zam thought about Yelena and Slink, two ghosts from his past. He was sure they were in Heaven; he just wasn't sure how they got there. 'Um, I don't know.'

'Shouldn't someone be here to help me?' the girl said, 'like an angel or something?'

'I guess.'

'You guess? You mean you don't know that either?'

'No, I'm sorry, I'm not much help.'

The spirit girl looked down at herself again. 'Where did the bowling ball come from?'

Zam pointed at the scaffolding. 'It came from up there.' He scanned the area, looking for the grey figure, but he couldn't see it anywhere.

The spirit girl looked up at the scaffolding. 'Someone was bowling up there?'

'I don't think so,' Zam said, unsure what to say and what to hold back. 'There was a figure up there, earlier. It was… I don't think it was human.'

'Not human?'

'There are creatures in this world that are not like us. More like creatures from fiction.'

'Ghosts, you mean?'

'Yes, ghosts… and others.'

'What, like aliens?'

'I don't know about aliens, but there are… zombies.'

'You've seen a zombie too?'

'No, but I've heard about one living in Edinburgh.'

The spirit girl put her head in her hands. 'This can't be happening to me.'

Zam remembered he was holding the severed finger and quickly put it in his pocket. 'I'm really sorry you... died. I'm sure someone will be here to help you soon.'

The spirit girl turned towards Zam. 'Do I know you?' she asked. 'You seem, familiar.'

'I don't think so. You seem familiar too, but I don't think we've ever met.'

'Now we will never meet.'

'No, that's not true. This is us meeting, right now.'

'But I'm dead.'

'Yeah, but you are the same, in a way.'

'What do you mean?'

'You are thinking the same way you thought before you died, right?'

The spirit girl studied Zam for a moment. 'Other than I now believe in ghosts, I guess I am thinking the same things, yes.' She buried her head in her arms again.

Zam could still see her face through her translucent arms.

'I'm still dead though.'

Zam looked around, searching for an angel or a light she could follow, but there was nothing. 'Why does God do this to people?'

'What?'

'I don't know... always keep us hanging on a thread.'

'Maybe that's why I'm stuck here like a ghost, I don't believe in God.'

Zam bit on his nail. 'No, I'm sure it's not that. I don't think you have to believe in Him to... No, it's not that.'

'What is it then? Why am I stuck here like this?'

'Maybe you have unfinished business,' Q said. 'I knew another ghost who had to stay amongst the living until he grew younger.'

The spirit girl's eyes widened. 'There is another ghost standing behind you,' she said. 'It's holding a meat cleaver. And its eyes, they look... wild. It didn't open its lips when it spoke.'

'That wasn't the ghost speaking.'

'No? Who was it then?'

'It was my wheelchair, Q.'

'Pleased to meet you,' Q said. 'I always wanted to be a ghost, but I don't think it's ever going to happen for me now.'

The spirit girl closed her eyes. 'This isn't happening,' she said, 'this is really not happening.' She opened her eyes again, but started to cry as soon as she did.

'Please don't cry,' Zam said, 'everything is going to be alright.' He turned away from her and started to wheel towards the house they were staying at. 'Follow me, I know someone who can help.'

'Where are you going?' the spirit girl asked, sobbing a little less.

'I'm staying here in this house for a few days. There is someone inside who understands more about these things than I do. She will be able to tell us why you are still here and not someplace else.'

'Wait.'

Zam stopped wheeling. 'What is it?'

'I'm frightened of knowing the answer to that question.'

Zam stared into the spirit girl's eyes and thought more than ever that he knew her from somewhere. 'I promise everything is going to be fine,' he said, thinking it was a promise he might not be able to keep.

The spirit girl blinked, and blinked again. Then she followed Zam, Q and the butcher ghost into the house with the purple front door and brass letterbox.

9

As they stepped into the hallway, Zam saw that it had bright white walls and a dark mahogany floor. The wide stairway curved upwards and its black, ornate balustrade stood out in the otherwise minimally furnished space. Despite its sanitary appearance, it smelled musty, as if it hadn't been opened up to fresh air for a number of weeks.

'Your grandson has found himself another shade,' Hestia said, as Zam entered the hallway with the others. 'He seems to like befriending creatures from the spirit world.'

'Napoleon?' Eli said, looking up from the note he was reading that was pinned to the wall above a telephone at the bottom of the stairs.

'I think something tried to kill me again,' Zam said. 'Instead of killing me, it killed...' he looked at the spirit girl, 'sorry, what's your name?'

The spirit girl was standing next to Zam, like she was afraid she would lose him if she didn't stay within inches of him. 'My name is Xara,' she said in a small voice. 'You are called Napoleon?' she asked, in a much louder voice.

Zam glanced at his grandfather, then back at Xara. 'Yes, but I like to be called Zam for short.'

'That's a cool name.'

'Your name is cool too,' Zam said.

'What kind of something just tried to kill you?' Hestia asked.

Zam looked thoughtful. 'It wasn't a doppelganger, it was kind of grey with black eyes. It seemed to be made up of rags. It kept flickering in the breeze all the time, like it was hollow. It threw a bowling ball at me, but it hit Xara instead.'

'I'm dead because of you?' Xara said.

'I think so,' Zam replied, 'sorry.'

'We need to get to Bonnyman as soon as possible,' Eli said. 'I don't want any more attempts made on Napoleon's life.'

'What about me?' Xara asked.

Hestia walked over to Xara. 'Child,' she said in her gentle, music-like voice, 'why didn't you follow the light?'

'What light?'

'The light that appeared when you passed over from the world of the living into the world of the dead.'

'I didn't see a light. I only saw... Zam,' she said.

Hestia looked from Xara to Zam and back again. 'Did you know him before today?'

'I've never seen him before in my life.'

'Hestia, we haven't got time for this,' Eli said.

'My God I'm dead. I'm really dead!' Xara, said, weeping once more.

Zam went to touch Xara's hand, but his hand passed straight through hers. He pulled back a little, until he hovered just above her hand. 'Don't cry, Xara, we'll figure this out.' He remembered what Hestia said about thinking of his hand being like a ghost hand. He tried again and this time his hand didn't pass through Xara's when he touched it.

Xara looked down at Zam. 'Why are you being so kind?'

'You'd do the same for me, right?'

'I think I'd run a mile if I saw a ghost.'

Zam grinned. 'I remember a ghost who did the same thing when he first saw another ghost.'

'You know other ghosts apart from me and that one?' she said, pointing towards the butcher ghost who stood at the opposite side of Zam, seemingly uninterested in anything they were saying.

'I see ghosts all the time, but not all of them are like you. I try not to speak to most.'

'What about him?'

Zam looked at the butcher ghost. 'I haven't made my mind up about him yet.'

Xara stared at Zam's hand touching hers. 'I can't feel you. And I can't smell anything or taste anything in my mouth. All I can do is see things and hear things.'

Zam bit his lip. 'We need to call the police,' he said.

Almost as soon as he uttered the words, a siren sounded outside.

'Looks like someone has already called them,' Q said.

'We can't get involved with the police,' Eli said, clenching and unclenching his fist.

Zam turned towards Grandfather. 'But I saw what happened.'

'How do you suppose you are going to explain to the police that you saw a flickering figure with black eyes kill this young girl with a bowling ball?'

Before Zam could answer, Jha came racing down the stairs. 'There's a police car and an ambulance outside,' he gasped.

Hestia stretched out her hand and gently placed it on Xara's shoulder. 'I know it is difficult for you to come to terms with what has happened to you, child, but I am certain help will arrive soon.'

'You mean an angel will come for me?'

'Yes, that's as good an explanation as any I can think of.'

'Why didn't someone or something come to help her as soon as she died?' Zam asked.

'I don't know,' Hestia said.

'Who are you talking to?' Jha asked.

'Xara,' Zam said.

'Xara?'

'The ghost standing next to me.'

'We have another ghost amongst us as well as the psychopath ghost?' Jha gasped.

'Yes,' Zam turned towards Hestia. 'Xara seems to be hiding herself from Jha.'

'I am?' Xara said.

Hestia sighed. 'Humans are not supposed to see spirits. Those with clairvoyant blood seem to be the exception.'

'Then why do some of us have clairvoyant blood and others don't?'

'You need to ask God that particular question, I cannot answer it in His place.'

Xara suddenly went rigid. 'Oh my God, what about my parents? My sister? Will they be able to see me?'

'It is unlikely, child,' Hestia replied.

'I need to see them now.'

'Where do they live?' Zam asked.

'Next door.'

Zam shuffled nervously in his seat. 'Which side, the house to our left or the house to our right?'

Xara pointed to her right. 'That side.'

'That's where I saw the creature on the scaffolding,' Zam said.

He remembered the finger in his pocket and he pulled it out. 'I think it left this for me to find,' he said to Hestia.

Hestia looked at the finger without touching it. 'It seems you now have a wraith wanting to take your life as

66

well as a doppelganger.' She turned towards Xara. 'Are your parents and sister at home?' she asked.

'Yes,' Xara replied, 'why, what's wrong?'

Hestia frowned. 'We need to get to them before the wraith does,' she said, 'else, your family will be a family of ghosts.'

Eli wanted to go with them, but Hestia told him he had to stay with Jha. She said Jha couldn't go next door because he was untutored in the way of the supernatural, he would be a liability.

'Fine,' Eli said, 'Napoleon stays here too.'

'Grandfather, I have to go with Hestia,' Zam said, 'I need to experience the supernatural because the supernatural comes looking for me every day of the week. You said yourself that I need to learn from Hestia.'

Eli sighed deeply, and then hugged Zam. 'Be careful,' he said, 'and make sure you do whatever Hestia tells you to do.'

Zam was saddened to see how old Grandfather looked and how easily he gave in these days. It seemed as if he was ageing a full year every day of the week since his return from the underworld. He looked tired and worn out, like he was about to give up on something. 'I'll be fine, Grandfather.'

Eli patted Q's armrest. 'Look out for him, Q.'

'Don't worry,' Q said, 'I won't allow anyone to turn him into a ghost. They will have to make me a ghost before that ever happens.'

Eli sighed, but said no more as Xara hurriedly led them through a doorway at the end of the hall that opened up into an expansive lounge.

'This is the quickest way,' she said, walking like she was gliding through the lounge until she reached a pair of French doors at the far side of the room. As she hurriedly attempted to open the doors, her hands passed straight through the door handles. Turning around in frustration, she watched as Zam quickly made his way to her side, opening the doors for her. Without a word, she stepped through the doorway into the patio area at the rear of the house with Zam following close behind. A small brick wall, no more than two feet high, divided the two properties. Xara didn't even attempt to jump over the wall, she just walked straight through it.

'How am I...' Zam started to ask Q

Before he finished asking the question, Q tilted backwards in a wheelie, and at the same time his chassis started to lengthen until half of the wheelchair was on one side of the wall and half on the other. Once in that position, he tilted in the opposite direction so that his front wheels touched the ground on the other side of the wall, and his rear wheels were raised. His chassis then began to shrink to its normal size, until the entire wheelchair was positioned on the other side of the wall. Q then lowered his rear wheels so that all four touched the ground.

'Oh,' Zam said.

'I do an amazing stunt like that and all you can say is *Oh*?' Q said.

Hestia vaulted the wall in one easy stride and landed next to Xara, who stood at the French doors to her family home. She didn't attempt to open the doors this time; she simply stepped through them and then turned around to face Hestia, who was unsuccessfully attempting to pull the doors open.

Xara pushed her head through the French doors and cocked it towards Hestia. 'Father is always losing his keys,' she said. 'That's why he had these special handles made. They don't need keys. Pull the handles apart, and then push them downwards.'

Hestia did as Xara said and the doors opened. 'That's so clever,' she said, smiling at Xara.

'Father designed them himself,' Xara said, as she quickly turned around and stepped further into the house.

Hestia and Zam slowly followed her inside, more wary to danger than Xara. The house was silent, yet Zam felt a tension inside that was palpable. The first room they entered was identical in size and shape to the lounge in the house where they were staying, but the room felt different, this room felt like it was suspended in time. A hardback book lay open and discarded on one of the two couches that faced each other in front of the fireplace. Zam could smell coffee and toasted teacakes. Seeing the tray of cups and plates on the table between the couches, he guessed the drinks and food had recently been prepared. Someone had been watching a movie on the large screen TV. Edward Scissorhands was frozen on the screen where the movie had been paused, with a look of melancholic bemusement on his pale face.

'Do you still have combat mode?' Zam whispered to Q.

'Yes,' Q replied, in a voice Zam could barely hear, 'and before you ask, yes, I am set in combat mode.'

'Great. Arm your lasers.'

'That might not be such a good idea,' Q replied. 'Remember what happened the last time you used lasers in a house, you nearly killed everyone inside.'

'Good point. What do you suggest?'

'I'm armed with miniature, ninja, shuriken, throwing stars. These babies are a little different to the norm. Once they bite into something they dig in and continue to spin until whatever it is they have bitten into is severed.'

'Where does Grandfather get the inspiration for all this lethal weaponry?' Zam asked, as they walked across the lounge and into the hallway.

'I'm not sure, maybe it has something to do with all those wildlife documentaries he watches.'

Zam looked up ahead and saw Xara standing by a

closed door, listening to something he could not hear. He pulled on Hestia's arm as she watched Xara.

'The finger is moving around in my pocket,' he said. 'I have a feeling something bad is about to happen.'

'The wraith is nearby,' Hestia replied.

As if to confirm her statement they heard a loud voice coming from behind the door Xara stood next to: 'Life is full of choices and you get to make a really special choice today, young one.'

Xara immediately stepped through the door and disappeared out of view.

Hestia and Zam moved towards the door. Hestia opened it and they entered the room, finding themselves in a study which had three walls lined with books. Zam saw the wraith standing behind a young girl, six or seven years old. She sat in a rocking chair next to a tall window. Directly opposite the chair were a man and a woman sitting side-by-side on a small, leather settee.

Every part of the wraith trembled, like leaves in the breeze, even though there was no breeze in the room. It had no facial features, other than its black eyes, which gave away nothing of what it felt. Unblinking, they were like puddles of water in the night, reflecting nothing but starlight.

'Sorry for the, umm, accident,' the wraith said to Xara, while it watched Zam and Hestia enter. 'I never meant to cause you any harm.'

'Mum? Dad?' Xara said, ignoring the wraith and rushing to her parents.

'They cannot hear you,' the wraith said gently, 'or see you for that matter. You are dead to them now, child.'

The wraith's captives looked as confused as they did frightened, turning their gaze from the wraith to Zam and Hestia and back again.

'Who sent you after Napoleon?' Hestia asked the wraith.

The wraith's dark eyes studied Hestia for a short while. 'You are not a fragile,' it said.

'No, I am not, now tell me who sent you, then leave this place. You do not belong here.'

Xara walked over to the girl on the seat. 'Beth, can you see me?'

Beth stared at the floor, obviously too frightened to look at the wraith or anything else in the room.

'Who are you to tell me where I do and do not belong?' the wraith said.

Hestia went to move towards the wraith, but stopped when it placed a hand around Beth's neck. 'That does not concern you,' she said.

'As this does not concern you either,' the wraith said, bending into Beth and removing its grip from her neck, before resting both of its bony hands on her shoulders. 'When the clock strikes 2:00,' it said to Beth, 'I want your decision or both of them will die.'

Staring at the wraith's left hand, Zam saw a stump where its index finger should have been, and knew then that the severed finger moving around in his pocket belonged to the wraith. Turning towards Xara's parents, he noticed for the first time two bowls of water on the floor. Her parents had their bare feet inside the bowls. An electric carving knife had been placed in one of the bowls and an electric toaster was placed in the other. Both power cables from the devices led to a double socket attached to an extension cable. The extension cable was plugged in at the socket next to where the wraith now stood.

Xara's parents stared at first the wraith and then their daughter sitting opposite. 'It's okay, Beth,' her father said, 'it's not your decision to make, it's mine. I love you very much. Now say my name, say my name before it is too late.'

Before Beth responded, Xara lunged at the wraith, but her hands went straight through it.

The wraith went to grab hold of Xara's neck and its hands didn't go straight through her. 'You may be a ghost,' it said, 'but I can still hurt you.' Lifting Xara off the floor, it squeezed her neck tightly. Xara started to make choking noises as she tried to wrench herself from the wraith's grip. The wraith remained unaffected by her efforts and continued to choke her.

'Hit that thing with everything you've got,' Zam ordered Q.

'I thought you'd never ask,' Q said in his driest Clint Eastwood voice, as a shuriken flew from his armrest.

The spinning star hit the wraith just below its elbow

74

and continued to spin until the wraiths lower arm was severed from its upper arm. Black liquid, that may have been blood but looked like an oil spill, spurted from the stump where the arm was no longer attached, while the hand around Xara's neck loosened its grip on her and dropped to the floor.

Momentarily stunned, the wraith quickly regained its composure and began to giggle in a way that no creature should ever giggle. 'That's a finger you owe me and now an arm too,' it said to Zam. Then it bent down, just as the clock chimed 2.00 and pressed the switch where the two plugs attached to the knife and toaster were connected.

'No!' Xara yelled.

It was too late for anyone to do anything, apart from Xara's mother, who grabbed hold of her husband's hand.

Before the electrical circuit breaker tripped out, the wraith began to spin around on the spot until it disappeared, leaving only the crackle of electricity and the smell of burning flesh.

11

Eli agreed to stay at the hospital with Beth until her relatives travelled up from Strathclyde to care for her. She was still in shock and could not tell the police what had happened. Eli explained to the police how they had heard screams coming from next door and when they entered the house at the back to investigate, Beth's parents were already dead and the murderer had fled. The police turned their investigation into a hunt for a serial killer who had not only killed Xara's parents, but two roofing contractors and Xara too.

'When your sister comes out of shock,' Eli said to Xara, 'we'll see what she remembers of the events. If she starts talking about a wraith, then it will be difficult for the police to believe her. They will think she is too traumatised to help them with the investigation. This is how it works with the supernatural, people are always more likely to believe in the unlikely, rather than the truth if it means they can rationalise things.'

'I can't do anything to help her,' Xara said 'She can't even see me. And my parents…'

Xara held onto Zam's hand and, strangely, it comforted him when he felt it prickle as she did. He didn't know what to say to comfort her. He guessed there wasn't anything he could say to make her feel better. They were in the visitor's seating area at the hospital. Zam hated hospitals; they always made him feel ill.

'Why aren't my parents ghosts like me?' Xara asked. 'I never saw a light or an angel take them away.'

Hestia shrugged her shoulders. 'I'm afraid there are no fixed rules after death, Xara. Each individual must take their own path.'

'I hope their path has taken them to a better place than mine.'

Zam tensed at Xara's words. He understood why she thought she wasn't in a good place, but he was getting used to having her around. He liked having her close.

'I will make sure your sister is well cared for,' Eli said, 'and I'll try to explain to her about the supernatural event she has just experienced when she is stronger. I don't want her thinking she is crazy.'

'Thank you,' Xara said, leaving Zam's side and attempting to hug Eli, but finding her arms passed straight through him.

'How did the wraith manage to grab hold of Xara?' Zam asked. 'She couldn't grab hold of the wraith.'

'She could have touched the wraith,' Hestia replied, 'if she stopped thinking like a ghost.'

Xara left Eli and stood next to Zam. 'How do I do that?' she asked.

'You will learn in time, if you remain a ghost,' Hestia said.

Zam went to touch Xara's hand again, but he forgot to think of his hand as a ghost hand and it passed straight through her.

Xara turned towards him. 'I felt your hand then,' she said.

'I can feel yours too. You're not as cold as Slink used to feel. His touch was like ice.'

'I feel like ice inside,' Xara said. 'I feel like my whole world has collapsed.'

'I'm sorry.'

'It's not your fault.'

'It feels like it is. Terrible things happen to people around me.'

'That seems to be the way of the gifted,' Hestia said.

'The gifted?' Zam said.

'Those who walk both sides of the line between life and death.'

'Why are they called gifted? Why not call them "the ones not to befriend"?'

Hestia ignored Zam and turned to Xara. 'Your world will change in time.'

Xara shook her head from side to side. 'I'm a ghost.

My parents are dead and I don't know where they are. My sister is alive and I know where she is, but she can't see or hear me. And I'm in a world where wraiths exist alongside ghosts and zombies. Right now, I'm terrified about any more changes in my world.'

Hestia looked from Xara to Zam and back again, but she remained silent.

Zam broke the silence. 'I remember you once said only the very strong or the very old could deny the light and remain in our world as a ghost. You said there wasn't a word for the strength you talked about in human language. You called it *zigg* in your language. Is that why Xara has remained behind? Has she got this *zigg* thing inside her?'

'I think she is full of determination and sentience, yes,' Hestia said. 'Yet I think it is more than *zigg* keeping her here. I think her being here has something to do with you.'

'What do you mean?' Zam asked, a little uncomfortable.

'Seeing you two together, there seems to be… a connection.'

'What kind of connection?' Xara asked.

'There isn't a word for it in your language.'

'What's the word for it in your language?'

'*Fengzy*,' Hestia said.

'What does *fengzy* mean?'

'It is to do with soul, with essence. It is a rare thing in this life, but not so rare in the afterlife.'

'I don't understand,' Zam said.

'You will in time,' Hestia replied, leaving it at that.

'I think I know what you mean,' Q said. 'I think I have a similar relationship with the girl of my dreams.'

'You have a girlfriend?' Hestia asked.

'No, he doesn't,' Zam replied. 'When he says "girl of his dreams", he literally means a girl he sees in his dreams. She is a bomb disposal unit.'

'Oh,' Hestia said.

'I share a special relationship with her,' Q said. 'Even though we only meet in my dreams, it's like we are still in perfect synchronicity. I think it has something to do with *fengzy*.'

'I'd like to think you are right, Q,' Zam said.

Hestia smiled, and then turned towards Eli. 'It is time we left,' she said. 'Is there anything you want from me before I leave?'

'Keep Napoleon safe,' Eli said.

Zam watched his grandfather carefully. It looked like he wanted to say more, but he didn't. Hestia suddenly kissed him on the cheek. Zam had never seen her do that before. It left him puzzled, wondering what kind of relationship his grandfather had with Hestia. After Zam said his goodbyes, they left Eli and Jha at the hospital with Xara and got a taxi back to the house. The butcher ghost came with them. He sat in the front passenger seat of the taxi, seemingly oblivious to everything going on around him. When they reached the house, Hestia said it was late and Zam needed to rest. They would confront Isaac Bonnyman in the underworld below the streets of Edinburgh the next day, and he needed to be sharp for the encounter.

Zam didn't argue: he felt drained.

Before they slept, Hestia prepared supper. She found some Caerphilly and a jar of pickles in the fridge, as well as a fresh loaf of bread that the housekeeper had left in the kitchen for them. She cut the bread into thick slices and toasted it with the cheese on top in the large range, spreading pickles on afterwards. Zam made hot chocolate drinks for them and when everything was ready, they sat opposite each other at the large kitchen table.

The toast was delicious, Zam didn't realise how hungry he was until he started to eat. He didn't feel like talking, but he had a question that had been burning in his head for some time. 'How did my grandfather get involved with the supernatural?'

Hestia looked as though she was enjoying supper as much as Zam and he didn't think she was going to answer.

'He helped me one night when he was very young,' she eventually said.

'How did he help you?'

'He stopped my father beating me with his cane.'

'Mandrake Ackx was beating you? Why would he do that?'

'He has lived too long for it not to have had some effect upon his temperament.'

'Are you saying he is crazy?'

'In a way, yes. All creatures of the underworld are psychotic in one form or another, especially those with changeling blood running through their veins.'

Zam had even more questions burning inside his head now. 'I thought your father was a wyte?'

'He is part wyte, part changeling.'

'What about your mother?'

'She was all changeling and also clairvoyant. Her seer blood does not run as strongly through my blood as it did hers though.'

'Where is she now?'

Hestia blinked rapidly. 'I do not know. She has been missing for a long time.'

'I have the same problem with my parents,' Zam said a moment later. 'They have been missing since I can first remember.'

'I'm sure there is a good reason for that.'

'Why are you so sure? Do you know them?'

'Not as well as I'd like to know them.'

Zam took a sip on his hot chocolate. 'They are not good parents. It's not their fault; I don't think they were ever meant to be parents.'

'I'm sure they are proud of you.'

Zam wanted to change the subject, thinking about his parents always made him feel uncomfortable. 'How can there be an underworld full of creatures like you and mankind not know about it?'

'We keep ourselves to ourselves. Most of the time.'

'Why?'

'Because God wants it that way.'

Zam finished eating before he asked another question. 'How did Grandfather stop Ackx from beating you with his cane? And how did he see you if you are supposed to keep yourselves to yourselves?'

Hestia smiled at Zam and he wasn't sure he liked her smiling at him. It wasn't an evil kind of smile; it was more an affectionate smile. He still wasn't sure he liked it.

'Your grandfather has always been a daydreamer and sometimes, when you dwell in that realm, you see things you shouldn't see. Father and I came into your world to observe a Perseids storm, a meteor shower that is best observed at pre-dawn – a time and event most humans miss. It is curious how humans search for beauty, yet miss so much right on their doorstep. Not your grandfather, though, he has always had a curious eye. That night he was the only human around. I still do not know why we had not seen him until the moment when he threw the stone at my father.

'He threw a stone at Ackx?'

'Yes, he hit him dead centre on his forehead.'

'He throws stones when we are by the riverside. He always manages to throw further than me and hit the target more times.' Zam took a deep breath. 'Your father was beating you purely because he is crazy?'

'He was annoyed that it clouded over just as the first shooting star appeared. He needed to vent his psychotic frustration in some way and beating me helped to ease his frustration.'

'I can't understand why you stay with him.'

'I told you before, parents are important to us.'

Zam shook his head from side to side. 'It's a shame that supernatural children are not as important to their parents. What did your father do when Grandfather hit him with the stone?'

'He was furious, at first. Then he began to laugh. Then he took your grandfather by the hand and led him into the underworld, where he kept him for more years than I care to remember.'

'How did Grandfather eventually escape?'

'He never escaped. My father let him return to your world when he was a grown man. And only then to work for him on various undertakings.'

'Grandfather's inventions you mean?'

'Yes and more.'

'What kind of more?'

Hestia took a long sip of her drink. 'It's late and we have an early start in the morning.'

'What kind of more?'

'The kind where if I told you, you would think differently of your grandfather.' Hestia stood up and looked down at Zam. 'He doesn't deserve that.'

'He is an old man. Do you love him?'

'He is not as old as me and yes, I am fond of your grandfather.'

'Are you going to marry him or something?'

'Do not worry. I will not take him away from you.'

'I don't mind,' Zam said, wondering if that was really true.

Hestia walked around the table until she was standing next to Zam. Then she bent down and gently kissed him on the top of his head. 'There are so many things in my life I regret,' she said. 'Meeting your grandfather is not one of them.'

Zam watched Hestia as she left the kitchen with even more questions buzzing in his head. Questions he wasn't sure he wanted answering.

12

Zam woke with a start. He sat up and let the pain wash over him. He had been dreaming about meteor storms and sunny afternoons by the river with Grandfather, skimming stones that sparked across the black surface of the water like rocks burning in the sky. The guest room on the ground floor had been prepared for him by the housekeeper, as there wasn't a stair lift to the upper floors. A lamppost located directly opposite the bedroom window shone through the thin material of the curtains and illuminated the room in a dreamy, white-orange glow. He glanced across at the clock. It was 3.22 am. The butcher ghost was sitting on Q. It was sleeping with its head rested against the cleaver, which it still held on to, as if it comforted the ghost to do so.

He was more surprised to see Xara sitting crossed legged on the easy chair opposite his bed. She stared at him with sorrowful eyes.

'I thought you'd still be at the hospital,' Zam said.

'There's nothing I can do there. Beth can't see me.'

'I'm sorry...'

'You don't have to keep saying sorry, it's not your fault. Nothing is your fault.'

Zam lowered his eyes. 'What are you doing here?'

'There is nowhere else for me to go,' Xara said, continuing to stare at Zam, making him feel uncomfortable. 'I like watching you sleep,' she added.

Zam's leg suddenly spasmed and he breathed in sharply. 'I need to do some leg stretches,' he said when the spasm subsided. Pulling himself out of the sheets, he lay back down on the bed and slowly pulled his right leg up until his heel almost touched his buttock. He held it there for a moment then straightened it until it lay flat on the bed again. He repeated the exercise with his left leg.

'That looks painful, can I help?' Xara said.

Zam stared at his legs. 'The nurse supports the underside of my leg when I do these at the hospital.'

Xara stood up and walked across to Zam. She put her hands under his thigh and tried to lift his leg. Her hand passed straight through his leg. She returned to the easy chair and slumped into it. 'I am worse than useless.'

Watching her, Zam had a thought. 'You're sitting in that chair.'

'Very observant, Zam.'

'I mean, you haven't passed through it, like you do everything else. You are actually sitting in the chair.'

Xara touched the arm of the chair. 'You're right, and I can feel it too. What does that mean?'

Zam thought for a moment. 'It means that you can

interact with things. We just have to figure out a way for you to do it all the time.'

'You really think I could do that?'

Zam sat up and turned towards Xara, resting on his elbow. 'I remember one ghost who could roll a stone on the floor without touching it. She must have used her thoughts to move the stone.'

'When I first sat in this chair I never thought about it, I just did it automatically without thinking. Maybe it has something to do with me not thinking.'

'Do you think you can go around without thinking all the time?'

Xara smirked. 'I used to act that way when I wasn't a ghost,' she said. She stopped smirking and her face looked sad again. 'Mum said I was a typical teenager going around with my head in the clouds.'

'I've never been that way. I've always had Grandfather to look after.'

'I like your grandfather. He is kind. He has stayed at the hospital watching over Beth all night.'

Zam thought about Hestia and what she'd said about Grandfather. He wondered what kind of things he had done that would make Zam feel different about him. He lay back down on the bed.

'It's too early in the morning to think,' he said, 'my head hurts as much as my legs do now.'

'When you were sleeping, you looked so peaceful, so happy. Were you dreaming?'

'Yes.'

'Tell me what you were you dreaming about?'

'I was skimming meteorites across the River Tyne at the quayside with my grandfather.'

'I'd like to dream something like that but I can't sleep. I don't think I will ever dream again.'

Zam stared at the butcher ghost. 'He looks like he is sleeping. Maybe he is dreaming too. I wonder what a ghost dreams about.'

'I'll tell you if I ever manage to sleep and dream again. In the meantime, will you dream for me and tell me about your dreams when you wake each morning?'

Zam nodded his head. 'All right, but I'll only tell you about the good dreams.'

'No, tell me about the bad dreams too,' Xara said.

'Why would you want to know about those?'

'Because they are your dreams, they are part of who you are.'

Zam closed his eyes. 'What do you want me to dream about tonight?'

Xara thought for a moment. 'Can you dream about me and you skimming meteors across Lake Windermere? It's one of my favourite places.'

Zam smiled with his eyes closed. 'Okay,' he said, 'just for you I'll give it a go.'

Xara stared at a golf ball that had been left on the floor underneath the dressing table. She tried to make it roll without touching it. After a number of unsuccessful attempts, she gave up. 'Do you think there's a connection between us Zam, like Hestia said?'

Zam opened his eyes and stared at the ceiling. 'I don't know. There's definitely a connection between Grandfather and Hestia, though. She can feel when he is upset, even when she is miles away.'

'That's cool. How do they do it?'

'I'm not sure. I think it is some form of telepathy.'

'Should we try to feel each other's emotions?'

'I was trying to sleep...'

'Sorry...'

'It's okay. We can have a go if you really want to.'

'How do we start?'

'I guess we close our eyes.'

'Okay, mine are closed.'

'Mine too.'

'Now what?'

'Umm, see if you can locate me with your mind. Try to read my mind and I'll do the same.'

They remained silent for a while and Zam almost fell asleep he was so tired.

'I can't feel anything,' Xara finally said, startling him a little.

'Me neither.'

'I don't think this is going to work.'

'Me neither.'

'You should sleep.'

'Okay. Goodnight, Xara.'

'Xyz.'

'What did you say?' Zam said, sitting up.

'Xyz.'

'Why?'

'I don't know, it just came into my head. Why?'

'I was saying *Xyz* in my head.'

Xara opened her eyes and looked at Zam. 'Why were you saying Xyz?'

'I used to repeat it inside my head whenever I was getting bullied. It comforted me for some reason. Now I say it when I'm nervous or trying to think.'

'Are you nervous now or just trying to think?'

'Both.'

'What makes you nervous?'

'You.'

'Me? Why do I make you nervous?'

'Because I like you.'

Xara smiled.

'Maybe we really are connected in some way,' Zam said. 'You tapped into my head and *Xyz* came to your head.'

'I hope so. I hope it wasn't just a coincidence.'

'It wasn't a coincidence.'

'You should sleep, Zam.'

'Yes.'

'When you do, I am going to try and see inside your dreams.'

Zam closed his eyes and started snoring.

'Are you sleeping already?'

Zam laughed. 'No, I'm just messing with you. I don't think it will be long before I am sleeping, though.'

'Goodnight, Zam.'

'Goodnight, Xara.'

***

Xara stared at the golf ball while she waited for Zam to sleep. 'Xyz,' she suddenly whispered while moving her eyes from side to side, in an attempt to make the golf ball move too. At first, the golf ball wouldn't play, but eventually, after only a short while, it began to move from side to side, synchronised with Xara's eye movements. Xara smiled, wanting to show Zam her new trick. His breathing was steady now, like he was sleeping. She didn't want to disturb him. She closed her eyes and tried to look into Zam's mind, into his dreams. She couldn't see anything. 'Xyz,' she began to whisper again, repeating it over and over as she continued to search for Zam's dreams. Sometime later, she found him beside Lake Windermere. She tried to speak to him, but he couldn't hear her. He couldn't see her either. She thought about that for a while, as she watched him skimming meteors across the perfectly still surface of the lake. The meteors left a liquid trail of fire drops as they bounced across the lake and Xara thought she had never seen anything so beautiful. She stared at Zam again, suddenly realising his legs weren't broken: they were just like everyone else's. *Two things*, she thought, *two things she had seen in one dream that she had never seen the likes of before.*

One of those things more beautiful than the other.

13

Zam awakened early the next morning, quickly ate his breakfast and ordered a taxi which dropped them off on the Royal Mile. From there, they made their way to Warriston's Close and arrived at The Real Mary King's Close gift shop a short while later.

'The entrance to the underworld is in here,' Hestia said, as they stood outside a covered walkway that served as a café, with tables and chairs beneath it. A few people sat at the tables drinking coffee and eating pastries.

'Isn't there a ghost door we could use to take us to Bonnyman's underworld?' Zam said.

'Yes,' Hestia replied, 'it's inside.'

Zam followed her into the cafe with Xara by his side and the butcher ghost trailing along behind. As ever, the butcher ghost looked disinterested and Zam wondered why it continued to follow him around.

'I was dreaming last night,' Q said, as Zam wheeled him between the tables.

'What did you dream about?' Zam asked.

'I dreamt there was a ghost in the bedroom talking about skimming meteorites across Lake Windermere.'

'That wasn't a dream, Q, it actually happened,' Zam said.

'It did?'

'Yes.'

'If I wasn't dreaming then why did I see it as a dream?'

'Maybe you were day dreaming, thinking you were asleep.'

'Maybe I'm doing the same now. I don't know what I'm doing anymore. I feel so different.'

'You just need to get used to the new you. I'm sure it will come in time.'

'Do you like the new me?'

'Yeah, you are cool, Q. You have always been cool.'

'I'll take your word for it,' Q said.

'You seem much happier this morning,' Hestia said to Xara.

'I've been skimming meteors across Lake Windermere,' Xara said, 'with Zam, last night.'

Before Xara could speak again Zam quickly said, 'Can you teach Xara how to interact with things? So she can maybe open doors or push my wheelchair.'

'I can push myself,' Q said, 'and I don't like being called a wheelchair.'

'It would be great if you could teach me how to touch things like a normal person, Hestia,' Xara said.

Hestia gazed from Zam to Xara. 'I don't know. It

depends upon you, Xara. Not all ghosts can manipulate things that way.'

'Xara sat in a chair last night, I mean really sat in it, she wasn't hovering above it and she never sank into it.'

'Last night?' Hestia asked.

'Early this morning,' Zam replied, blushing slightly.

'I managed to move a golf ball with my eyes too,' Xara said.

'You had your eyes pressed against a golf ball?' Q asked.

'No,' Xara said. 'I moved my eyes backwards and forwards and the golf ball moved with the movements of my eyes.'

'How did you do that?'

'I have no idea, I mean, I think it's a telekinetic thing, but I don't know how I managed to become that way. Zam put the idea into my head.'

Q laughed. 'You don't have a head – you're a ghost.'

'He put it into my mind then.'

Hestia looked at Xara for a brief moment. 'Alright,' she said. 'I will try to help you.'

'Thank you, Hestia,' Xara said, 'thank you so much.'

The café opened up into a gift shop with a square shaped counter in the centre of the room. Zam looked around wondering how it would lead them to the underworld. 'They sell tickets to Edinburgh's underworld here?' he asked Hestia.

'Yes, but not Isaac Bonnyman's underworld,' Hestia

replied. 'Edinburgh's underworld City of the Dead is manmade.'

'That's right,' Xara said, 'there are any number of vaults and tunnels beneath the city that are already known and some believe more are still to be discovered.'

'We can get to Isaac's underworld via the tunnels beneath Edinburgh,' Hestia said.

'Let's get going then,' Zam said. 'I want to know what this zombie has to say about the doppelganger that's stalking me.'

Hestia led them to the counter where she asked for tickets to the City of the Dead underground tour.

'There is no wheelchair access,' the cashier told her, as she stared at Zam.

'That's not a problem,' Zam said, 'my wheelchair can hover.'

'Actually, I can do more than hover, Zam,' Q said. 'I can do this.'

Zam heard the familiar whine and hum of motors that Q made whenever he was about to transform. At first, he felt himself being raised and thought Q was about to transform into some kind of flying machine again, but when he felt himself standing upright, with his spine and legs supported by Q, he realised something else was happening.

'Try walking,' Q said when the transformation noise stopped.

Zam looked down at his legs and saw that Q had

moulded himself around the back of them like an exoskeleton. He had done the same from Zam's ankles to his shoulders, so that it looked like he was wearing a half suit of futuristic armour. Zam went to move his leg forwards and again, Q's motors hummed.

'I can sense your movements,' Q said. 'When your leg moves, I do too. Not only can I support you, I can also power 95% of the movements you make, so we don't have to rely on your leg muscles.'

The other people in the shop stared at Zam. Some of them took photographs of him.

'That's absolutely amazing,' a tall man dressed in a bright, flowery shirt and white shorts said. 'How did you do that?'

'That would be my grandfather,' Zam replied. 'He's an inventor.' He didn't think it would be wise to add that his grandfather's inventions also included underworld technology.

'He's more than an inventor, he's a genius,' the man replied.

'Yeah, I guess he's that too.'

Everyone in the shop started to gather around Zam, pointing and commenting about his metal suit that looked more like a robotic skeleton.

Zam hated the attention. 'When does the tour start?' he asked the cashier.

'In ten minutes, when the tour guide arrives,' she said.

Zam walked across to the queue at the door leading into

Edinburgh's City of the Dead and waited. Hestia joined him and Xara stood next to him. He tried to ignore everyone staring at him and commenting about Q's new form.

Xara leant into him and whispered into his ear. 'You seem to be a celebrity.'

As she spoke, Zam felt an incredible tingling sensation run down the length of his spine. Inside his head, Xara's voice echoed like he thought electricity would sound if it could speak. It was one of the most remarkable feelings he had ever experienced in his life. With his spine still tingling, he turned towards Xara.

'You don't have to whisper,' he said. 'Only we can see and hear you.'

'Sometimes I forget. I'm still not used to this ghost thing.'

'You've only been a ghost for a day.'

A dark shadow crossed Xara's face and she looked to the ground.

'Are you all right, Xara?' Zam asked.

'No. I've just remembered I'm dead and my mother and father are dead. I keep forgetting that too.'

Zam didn't know what to say and when the woman in front turned around and flashed him a curious look, he was relieved to think about something else.

'It's okay, I talk to myself all the time,' he smiled.

The woman smiled back, shaking her head and turned around to face the entrance to the City of the Dead.

Zam leant into Xara and whispered into her ear. 'It's me who needs to be more careful, people will think I'm crazy or something.'

Xara stood perfectly still without saying anything.

'What is it?' Zam asked, whispering into her ear again.

Xara closed her eyes. 'Just then, when you whispered into my ear, it felt like…like I was no longer a ghost. My neck and shoulders tingled and, for a moment, I could taste strawberries inside my mouth.'

'I felt something amazing when you whispered into my ear, too. I thought it was a ghost thing. I didn't think I'd have the same effect on you.'

'Maybe you should leave this conversation for a more private moment,' Hestia said.

Zam blushed.

Xara opened her eyes. 'Wow,' she said.

The door to the underground opened and a guide dressed as an 1800's pauper appeared. 'Welcome ladies and gentlemen,' she said. 'Follow me and we can get started.'

They followed her into a darkened lobby and when everyone was inside, she closed the door. As they settled, the woman gave the usual safety talk, looking Zam up and down as she did. Then they followed her down some crooked stairs and into a small antechamber.

'The underground world I am about to show you,' the guide continued, 'is made up of a number of streets buried beneath the city. This came about in the seventeenth century when the city council at the time were looking for a site where they could construct the Royal Exchange building. Mary King's Close and a number of other streets were deemed to be an ideal location. Instead of demolishing these streets, they were used as foundations for the new building above.'

Zam listened intently as the guide talked, taking in the smell of rubble and damp air, while gazing around at the cramped, dimly lit space. He tried not to think about the buildings above, how their weight could easily crumble the walls of the ancient street he now stood in and crush him in a burial chamber of soil and rubble. Being claustrophobic, Zam wondered how it was possible that he was always so easily talked into coming underground. Ever since the world of the supernatural had found him, it seemed that he spent most of his time underground where he felt most uncomfortable. If he had a choice, he would leave the underworld to the supernatural beings that seemed drawn to him for reasons he didn't understand. Seeing as he didn't have a choice, he confronted his fear and tried to distract his mind from what he was feeling. If he allowed his thoughts to wander down the path where his fear took him, he knew he would lose more than just his mind. Taking a deep breath, he stared at the guide and listened to her talk, using her voice to block out thoughts of nightmarish constriction. When the guide finished talking, she headed for a low entranceway at the far end of the space, telling them to follow her.

'Stay here,' Hestia said, as she watched the others leave.

When they were alone, Hestia turned towards Xara. 'Do you see the door?' she said.

'Yes,' Xara replied, 'over there by the mannequin with the pointy beak.'

Zam looked over to where Xara indicated and saw a black-cloaked mannequin wearing a mask with an elongated beak. It was staring down at a small, child-like mannequin lying on its back. The child-mannequin suffered from the plague. The guide had told them that doctors wore the beak masks during the plague. They filled the beak with a variety of aromatic herbs in the belief it would save them from the disease. In all likelihood it would have masked the odour of death, but it would not have been a saviour from the plague.

Zam could not see the door. He didn't expect to see it.

'The ghost door is invisible to human eyes,' Hestia continued, 'only supernatural beings can see ghost doors.'

'I see other things,' Xara said. 'Things I didn't see when I was not a ghost. There are colours I can't describe.'

'Slink used to see scents rather than smell them,' Zam said.

'Slink?' Xara asked.

'He was a ghost I used to know.'

'Concentrate on the door,' Hestia said.

'Where does the door lead?' Xara asked.

'It leads to the underworld. The real underworld.'

'Why did we have to come all the way to Edinburgh?' Zam asked. 'Why couldn't we just enter the underworld like we did in Newcastle?'

'The underworld of Newcastle and Edinburgh are connected – just like they are also connected to the underworld of Dublin and Paris and more – but the underworld is vast. To get from one city to another via the underworld would take ten times longer than if we travelled through the ghost doors of your world.'

'Are you saying that supernatural creatures use our world as a short cut to reach different areas of the underworld?'

'Yes, that is one of the reasons they spend time in your world.'

'What are the other reasons?'

'Primarily to cause mischief.'

'Is the underworld hell?' Xara asked.

'No child, it is not hell. Not in the way you think of hell.'

'Does hell really exist?'

'Yes.'

'Are there doorways into hell too?'

'The doorways into hell are all inside the mind.'

'So they are only imaginary and not real?'

'They are everything you can imagine and as real as the thoughts you are now thinking.'

Zam laughed. 'You have to get used to Hestia and her ways, Xara. Not only is she an old adult, she is a very old adult. She never gives you a straight answer.'

'Try and open the door, Xara,' Hestia said, ignoring Zam.

Xara moved across to the ghost door and as soon as her hand touched the wall where the ghost door was located, it became visible to Zam. She tried to grab the door handle, but her hand passed straight through it.

'Do not think like a ghost,' Hestia said. 'Think like you are someone who can twist the knob with your thoughts.'

Xara concentrated on what Hestia said and instead of using her hand, she visualised the door-knob turning inside her thoughts.

It still didn't turn.

'Use your hand if it will help you to visualise.'

Placing her hand on the door-knob, Xara twisted it, while at the same time visualising the door knob twisting too. This time it did turn and Xara began to visualise the door opening as she pulled it towards her. When the door was fully open, she turned around and faced Hestia. 'I did, it,' she said. 'I actually opened a ghost door.'

'Yes, now you are becoming more than a ghost. Now you are becoming a shade.'

'A shade? What's the difference between a ghost and a shade?' Xara asked.

'A shade can open ghost doors,' Hestia replied.

'Oh,' Xara said.

Zam laughed. 'I warned you about what she's like,' he said.

'I think I'd prefer to be a shade than a ghost,' Q said.

'It's time to get serious,' Hestia said. 'Time we discovered what Isaac knows about rogue doppelgangers and wraiths.'

Zam looked past Xara into the open doorway, wondering how Isaac Bonnyman's underworld was going to compare to Mandrake Ackx's underworld. He wondered if it was going to change him like Ackx's underworld had changed him beneath the streets of Newcastle. There was only one way to find out, and watching Xara walk through the ghost door, he wondered too, how it would change her.

14

Zam didn't like being part of an exoskeleton. It felt like he was more of a freak than ever and before he went through the ghost door, he asked Q to morph back into a wheelchair. As they entered the doorway and the door closed behind them, Zam saw that Bonnyman's underworld was like London in 1977. London by the docks to be more precise, with *The Clash* singing 'London Calling'.

'This is the underworld?' Xara said.

'This is *The Clash*,' Zam said, 'this is actually *The Clash* performing 'London Calling' live!'

'How can we be in London?' Xara asked. 'How can we have gone back in time?'

'We are in an underworld neutral zone,' Hestia said. 'In neutral zones, the underworld becomes a thought, an image from whoever is present at the time.'

'I kinda had *The Clash* playing in my mind as we walked through the ghost door,' Zam said. 'You know, like you have music inside your head when your mind wanders.'

'You do that too?' Xara said. 'And you like *The Clash*?'

'I love *The Clash*. I want to be like Joe Strummer or Mick Jones.'

'I prefer techno music,' Q said. '*Kraftwerk* and Gary Numan are more to my tastes. I always wanted to be like C3PO or a horse. Did I ever tell you that Zam?'

'Yes, Q. You told me before that you wanted to be a horse, amongst other things.'

As they stood side by side watching *The Clash* perform, it started to snow, sleet-like at first, then heavier, until flakes the size of large hands fell to the ground and, as the snow landed, it began to change everything. The Thames disappeared first and then the boat *The Clash* were performing on faded, though *The Clash* remained standing on a snow-covered clearing with leafless, stark trees in the background. Eventually, even *The Clash* disappeared and the landscape changed from London in 1977 into a bleak snow covered moor as the last chords of 'London Calling' faded into the sound of wind blowing all around.

'Hestia,' a voice behind them said, 'you come into my world unannounced.'

Zam turned around and saw a tall, broad man before him. He stood with his hands in the pockets of the greatcoat he wore. His gaunt face held the expression of unending pain and, on closer inspection, Zam saw that the man's skin was too white, almost the colour of the snow that fell all around him, like it was devoid of melanin. As if his skin was dead. The only colour on the man's face was from the black rings around his eyes. Zam suddenly realised it wasn't his skin that was black; it was dark because his eyes were sunken into his head, like he didn't really have any eyes, just the eye sockets of a skull. The man did have eyes though and Zam shivered, not sure if it was because of the cold or the intense eyes that stared back at him like they could see into Zam's darkest secrets.

'I do so only because a friend's life is in danger, Isaac,' Hestia said.

'What has that got to do with me?'

'A Pict doppelganger put his life in danger.'

Bonnyman stared at Hestia with eyes that showed nothing of what he was thinking. 'Come with me,' he said, turning around and becoming almost lost to them as he walked into the snow storm.

They hurriedly followed, attempting to keep up with Bonnyman, whose surefootedness – for a zombie – surprised Zam. Feeling like he was about to freeze to death, Zam asked Q if he had anything he could use to keep him warm.

'I'm a high-tech personnel carrier and war machine,' Q said, 'not an electric heater.'

Q's abruptness surprised Zam, but he said no more and instead zipped his jacket up to the top of his neck. It hardly made a difference. He looked across at Xara, barely able to make her out as her form melded into the falling snow. Just as he felt like his fingers were going to drop off in the cold air, his spirits lifted when he saw a light up ahead. As they approached the light, he saw it came from a large canvas tent that blew in the wind, straining against its fastening as if it was about to be blown away. Bonnyman stopped at the tent, opened a flap and stepped inside without looking back to see if they were still there.

When they reached the tent, Hestia quickly opened the flap and they wordlessly entered. It was incredibly calm inside the tent, as if the canvas it was constructed from had sapped the wind's will to gust and blow. A log fire burned in the centre and a number of scatter cushions were placed around the blaze. Zam was grateful for the warmth it provided. Bonnyman sat by the fire and indicated for them to do the same when they entered. Zam unbuckled Q's strap and slid onto the floor next to Hestia, warming himself by the flames of the fire.

'Your ghost doesn't like me,' Bonnyman said.

The butcher ghost stood next to the tent flap with its arms crossed. It still held onto the meat cleaver and it stared across at Bonnyman with baleful eyes.

'I don't think he likes anyone,' Zam said.

'The ghost follows *you*?' Bonnyman sounded surprised, as if he expected the ghost to be with Hestia rather than Zam.

'Not all the time, sometimes it disappears and reappears later. I'm not sure what it wants from me.'

'It's attracted to your energy. All shades are the same. They want to be alive again.'

'Maybe that's why he is unsure of you.'

'What do you mean?'

'You are dead,' Zam said in a flat voice, 'yet you are a zombie, not a ghost like him. I guess you don't have the same energy as me and it's confusing him.'

Bonnyman turned towards Hestia. 'Tell me about the boy,' he said.

'He is called Napoleon Xylophone,' Hestia said.

'He is the child who destroyed your father?'

Hestia nodded. 'Yes, and I am asking you to call off the Picts who are stalking him.'

'You think I have put a bounty on his head?'

'Who else but you commands Krackle and a shade wraith?'

'Krackle?'

'He tried to pull me into a mirror and absorb me,' Zam said, 'and the wraith, it killed Xara and her parents yesterday.' He nodded towards Xara, then pulled the wraiths finger from his pocket and showed it to Bonnyman. 'It left this, oh, and it's missing an arm too.'

Bonnyman looked at the finger Zam held onto and stared into his eyes. Zam wanted to turn away from the zombie's gaze, but held it anyway.

'You are really Xylophone?' Bonnyman said.

'He is,' Hestia replied.

Bonnyman turned his gaze back towards Hestia. 'I

know nothing of this,' he said. 'Krackle and the shade wraith are not acting on my instructions. Clearly, they are acting upon someone's though.' Bonnyman's eyes narrowed and became almost invisible in their shrunken sockets. 'And I need to find out who that someone is.'

Hestia studied Bonnyman for a moment and Zam thought that she must have been deciding whether or not to believe him. 'We need to find the shadow wraith,' Hestia finally said, 'it is our best chance of discovering who is controlling who.'

Bonnyman picked up a metal poker lying by the fire and began to move the embers at the heart of the fire back and forth. 'There is only one place a shadow wraith is likely to go if it is searching for replacement body parts. That would be the Wiccan coven near Lakura.'

'Can you take us there?'

'Yes, but we need to be quick. The wraith has a lead on us, we need to travel swiftly.' He looked at Zam. 'We should leave the boy here. He will slow us down.'

'Don't worry about me,' Zam quickly said. 'I can travel as swiftly as anyone else sitting around this fire.'

'Where is Lakura?' Hestia asked Bonnyman.

'It is this side of the great forest.'

'How long will it take us to get there?'

'Two days flying on the back of a wyrm. Is the boy capable of riding a wing mount?'

'I don't need a wyrm, whatever that is, I have a

wheelchair,' Zam said, looking across at Q, hoping he could still fly as well as he used to fly.

Bonnyman didn't look too convinced.

'Do not worry about Napoleon,' Hestia said. 'He is more resourceful than he looks.'

Zam felt offended at being told he didn't look very resourceful. Thinking about how cold it was outside, he pushed his resentment to one side. 'One problem I might have is the weather,' he said. 'I'm not sure I can survive for too long out there in the cold.'

'Leave the weather to me,' Bonnyman said, throwing the poker on the floor and standing up in one fluid movement that surprised Zam.

Bonnyman stared down at Hestia. 'This child really defeated your father?'

'Yes, he did,' Hestia said.

'Then why are you helping him?'

Hestia stood up and looked Bonnyman in the eyes. 'Because I think there is a good chance that he might stop me from going crazy.'

'That's reason enough,' Bonnyman said. 'I need to eat before we leave. If I do not feed, nothing will stop me from going crazy apart from eating you and the boy.' He walked into the shadows at the rear of tent, raised the lid of a large crate stored there and pulled out what Zam first thought was a baby. As he stared at the creature Bonnyman held, he realised it was not a child, it was more a cross between a monkey and a ravaged old man.

Bonnyman brought the creature up to his mouth and started to eat it. The creature did not make a noise or show any sign that it was distressed, which troubled Zam more than if it had screamed out in terror. Zam turned away from Bonnyman but the sound of him ripping flesh from the creature's bones and then chewing on that flesh made him feel nauseous.

'I need to leave,' Xara said. She turned away from them and moved to the edge of the tent where she walked straight through the canvas without opening the flap.

Zam lifted himself onto Q and moved to leave the tent too. When he pulled the flap aside, a brutish looking creature blocked his path. It was human in shape, but bestial in appearance, with clawed hands and skin that wouldn't look out of place on a dead reptile. The butcher ghost stood at Zam's side and held the cleaver as if it was going to use it on the creature blocking Zam's path. Zam turned towards Hestia looking for guidance. She shook her head indicating that he should remain in the tent. Wheeling himself back towards the fire, Zam stopped next to Hestia and stared into the flames attempting to ignore the sound Bonnyman made as he continued to eat the placid creature alive.

'What is that thing at the door?' Zam asked Hestia.

'A night gaunt,' Hestia said, without explaining any more.

When he finished eating, Bonnyman tossed the remains of the creature into a half-barrel located next to the crate. Pulling more creatures from the crate, he dropped them into a sack he picked up off the floor, knotted it and then slung it over his shoulder.

'Come,' Bonnyman said, 'I only have a day or so before I need to feed again. I can't take too many kriungs with me so we need to use that time wisely.'

Zam guessed that kriungs must be the name of his food supply. He stared at the sack Bonnyman carried on his back and wondered why the kriungs were so docile. There was no movement from the sack. They seemed to accept their fate like they didn't realise their fate ended with them being eaten alive. *Maybe they are drugged or held under some kind of underworld spell*, he thought.

When Bonnyman opened the tent flap the gaunt standing outside moved aside. Bonnyman exited the tent and the others followed him outside where Zam was relieved to see the storm had ceased. He remembered what Bonnyman had said about the weather and wondered if he had made the snowstorm stop. He wondered then if Bonnyman had made the storm start in the first place and if he had also been responsible for *The Clash* disappearing. He stared at Bonnyman as the zombie bent down and scooped up a handful of snow which he used to clean the blood off his hands and face. When he was finished, red-tinged snow lay all around his feet.

Bonnyman nodded to the gaunt and it entered the tent. It exited a brief moment later with the remains of the kriung the zombie had half-eaten in its arms. It disappeared behind the tent and Zam heard ferocious growls and yelps as if a pack of hyenas were fighting over food.

Bonnyman stared at Zam. 'We do not waste food here, unlike your world.'

'We don't eat food that's still alive,' Zam replied, 'unlike your world.'

Bonnyman turned away from Zam and raised his face to the sky. He placed his hands at both side of his mouth and howled into the underworld air like a wolf calling its companions to the hunt. The sound of the beasts feeding on the remains of the kriung behind the tent momentarily stopped as they howled in response before continuing to devour their carrion.

Zam stared into the sky and, at first, he didn't see anything. A moment later, he spotted a dark shape circling high above Bonnyman. The shape started to descend and the air around them swirled, blowing snow all around, as it finally hovered a few feet above them. Zam guessed the creature must have been the wyrm wing mount Bonnyman had spoken about earlier. Larger than any animal Zam had ever seen before, it was totally black, with wrinkled folds of skin. Sinewy and serpentine in form, its wing-span was twice its length. It made Zam feel incredibly vulnerable, like he was about to be eaten alive in the same manner as the kriung in the tent earlier.

Without taking his eyes off the wing mount, he

suddenly became worried that Q would not be able to keep up with the wyrm.

'Can you still fly like you did when you were the other wheelchair, Q?' he asked, nervously.

'No, not the same,' Q replied. 'I think I can fly faster than that.'

Zam smiled. 'Great, let's show this flesh-eating zombie and his poor excuse for a dragon how flying should be done then.'

'Zam,' Xara said as Q began to transform. 'What about me and your butcher ghost?'

Zam considered Xara's question, wondering if a ghost could fly. He quickly decided Xara wouldn't know how to fly yet, even if she could. There wasn't time to teach her, either. She would have to fly with him on Q. 'Can you make yourself wider, Q,' he said, 'so Xara can sit beside me?'

'I don't know,' Q replied, 'I can try.'

Zam wasn't concerned about the butcher ghost, he was sure it would find a way to follow him if it really wanted to. He wondered where it went when it disappeared. More so, he wondered why it kept following him and why it seemed to be protective towards him now. If he did lose the butcher ghost, he would certainly miss it.

Q's motors whined as he started to hover a few feet in the air. His wheels then slid downwards before flipping ninety degrees and disappearing beneath him. The motor noise was accompanied by the creak of alloy and carbon fibre as well as, Zam guessed, other underworld materials as Q's wheelchair form shifted into a flat, elongated flying machine similar in shape to a spearhead. Looking down at Q's liquid-like, reflective surface, Zam thought that Q must have been secretly spying on his dreams.

'That's a cool wheelchair you have, Zam,' Xara gasped.

'Yeah, but it isn't big enough for both of us to sit in,' Zam said. 'Q, is this as wide as you can go?'

'I'm sorry, I can't stretch any further,' Q said.

Hestia stepped away from them and quickly morphed into a wyrm that looked even blacker and nastier than Bonnyman's wyrm.

'You can ride on the back of Hestia,' Zam said, after she had finished shape-shifting.

'You seem to think I am some kind of mule, Napoleon,' Hestia said, in a voice that sounded nothing like how Zam expected a wyrm to sound. 'I seem to remember telling you before that no one rides on a changeling.'

'And I seem to remember riding a changeling that had morphed into an albino sabre-toothed tiger,' Zam replied. 'Xara is part of whatever it is we have got ourselves into. The wraith killed Xara and her parents. She deserves to know why all of this has happened.'

Hestia sighed heavily. 'Fine, but don't tell anyone I let her ride on me.'

Xara shook her head. 'I can't sit on Hestia, I'll fall straight through her.'

'Don't think about what you are doing,' Zam said. 'Remember the chair in my bedroom? How you sat on that without thinking.'

'I'll try,' Xara said, suddenly putting her arms behind her back and walking in a circle, while whistling *The Clash's* 'White Man in Hammersmith Palace'.

'Is that how you stop thinking,' Zam said, 'you whistle *Clash* songs?'

'I'm learning as I go along,' Xara, said, as she continued to whistle. A moment later, when she faced Hestia, she dashed to her side and attempted to climb onto her back, but fell straight through her, landing in the snow beneath Hestia's abdomen.

Hestia didn't laugh, even though she looked like she wanted to, as much as a wyrm could. 'Try to visualise your action before you do it, do the same thing you did when you opened the ghost door.'

Xara got up and stood next to Hestia, attempting to grab her skin so she could shimmy up Hestia's haunches, but her hands kept slipping straight through Hestia.

'Why don't you glide onto my back, instead of climbing up my side like that?'

'I can glide?' Xara asked.

'Of course you can,' Zam said laughing, 'didn't you know that all ghosts can glide?'

'You don't know that for sure, you are just mocking me, aren't you?'

'Maybe,' Zam said.

'I'll get you back for that, Zam, I never forget anyone who makes fun of me.'

Zam was about to answer when he noticed Xara's feet were no longer touching the ground. He continued to stare as she raised herself further from the ground until she was high enough to sit on Hestia's back. After remaining there for a brief moment, she started to sink downwards, as if she was going to end up on the floor again. Zam could see by her face that she was concentrating hard.

'Don't think about not being able to sit on Hestia,' Zam said. 'Try to think about flying on her instead. Or think about nothing at all.'

Xara closed her eyes. 'Do I feel heavy?' she asked Hestia.

'You are as light as a ghost feather,' Hestia said.

'As light as a ghost feather,' Xara repeated, as she became more stable and remained seated on Hestia's back without sinking into her. 'That's a great way of thinking about myself.' She opened her eyes and grabbed hold of the loose flesh around Hestia's neck. 'I think I can do this.'

'You can, Xara,' Zam said, 'and trust me, flying, real flying like this I mean, is the coolest fun ever.'

Xara winked at Zam and he smiled back at her, thinking a ghost wink was almost as cool as flying.

Without any visible direction from Bonnyman, his wyrm crouched down low on its haunches and the zombie grabbed hold of it, pulling himself up on its back.

Once he was seated, he kicked the side of the wyrm and it stood upright, lifted its head back and screeched out loud, until Zam thought his ears were going to burst. Spreading its wings wide, it slowly raised itself from the ground and then surged into the sky. Hestia followed suit and Xara whooped as they soared upwards.

Zam was about to ask Q to follow them when he heard movements behind. Turning around he saw the gaunt that had blocked his way out of the tent. It stared at him, looking hungry and standing on four paws rather than standing on its hind legs like it had at the tent flap. It was joined by a dozen or more identical looking creatures. All of them looked hungry. All of them had their teeth bared, and all of them slowly walked towards Zam.

The butcher ghost moved away from Zam and stood between him and the gaunts with the meat cleaver held prone in its hand. The gaunts stopped their advance and stared at the butcher ghost like he was their worst enemy and they were about to make him pay for past wrongs.

'Q, it's time we got out of here,' Zam said, grabbing hold of the joysticks in Q's armrests and pulling them backwards. Q instantly shot forwards, rising into the air at a steep incline. Zam looked down and saw the gaunts circling the butcher ghost. The butcher ghost turned around and around, swinging the meat cleaver at them but as soon as he had his back to one of the gaunts, it would snap at him with its ferocious jaws. Staring down at the battle below, Zam couldn't understand how the gaunts were able to bite the butcher ghost. Their teeth ripped ghost flesh away from him while they easily avoided his cleaver.

'We have to help him,' Zam said.

'We do?' Q said.

'Yes,' Zam answered, as he guided them back towards Bonnyman's camp.

'You said the ghost is a psychopath, why help it?'

'Because it feels like the right thing to do. Now tell me, what battle options have I got?'

'We have the usual lasers and shurikens,' Q answered, 'and we have electrical bolts and a flame thrower.'

'Arm the electric bolts,' Zam said.

'Electric bolts armed,' Q said.

When they were twenty metres or so from the gaunts, Zam took aim, pressed the buttons on top of the joysticks and watched as two electrical charges spiralled their way from the front of Q towards the gaunts below. The bolts hit the two nearest creatures and arced across to the ones standing beside them until all of the gaunts were connected and frozen in place in a ring of electrical charge.

'Quick, over here,' Zam shouted at the butcher ghost as he guided Q downwards towards the edge of the gaunts.

The ghost held onto its leg where it was bleeding ghost blood and started to hobble towards the ring of gaunts that surrounded it. Before it got any further, a charge of electricity sprang from the nearest gaunt and curled itself around the ghost and it too, stood frozen and twitching to the pulse of the energy that held it in place.

'That didn't go as planned,' Zam said. 'How do we discharge the electric current?'

'Like this,' Q answered, as a shuriken spun out of his fuselage and embedded itself in one of the trees next to the ring of gaunts.

Zam couldn't see the shuriken, but he could hear it spinning within the tree trunk and seconds later, the shuriken sliced through the trunk and then dropped harmlessly onto the floor at the other side. Zam heard a creaking noise and then watched as the tree slowly leant forwards until a loud crack sounded out and the tree fell at great speed onto the gaunts and the butcher ghost. As the tree fell, the electric energy holding the gaunts in place discharged along the length of the tree and they dropped to the floor, yelping and whining in agony.

'Over here,' Zam yelled at the butcher ghost.

The bleeding ghost looked up at Zam and began to limp over to him. 'Climb on,' Zam said, pointing to the front of the fuselage.

The butcher ghost climbed on top of Q and Zam tried to hold onto it, but he couldn't, and the ghost slid around on top of Q's fuselage. 'Take us away from here,' Zam said to Q as he looked back and saw the gaunts shaking off the effects of the electricity and staring at him, like *he* was now their worst enemy.

Q's propulsion system kicked in and they rose sharply from the ground, flying in the direction of Bonnyman and Hestia, who were now tiny black dots in the sky up above. Zam watched helplessly as the butcher ghost slid around on top of Q as they flew, until it eventually fell from the fuselage and plummeted towards the ground below. Before it hit the ground, it disappeared and Zam blinked, hoping to see it reappear safe on the ground somewhere. Scanning the area, he couldn't see the butcher ghost anywhere.

'It's a ghost, it can't die again,' Q said. 'I'm sure it will be all right.'

'Those creatures were ripping flesh from it and it was bleeding. I'm not so sure. Things are different in the underworld.'

'It did not hit the ground. It disappeared. Maybe it has just gone to the same place it goes whenever it leaves you.'

'I hope so,' Zam said. 'I'm getting used to having it around.'

'Even though it's a psychopath?'

'I'm not so sure it is a psychopath any more. It was protecting me, why would it do that if it was a psychopath?'

'I don't know and I don't know if you can trust it. If it comes back, I mean.'

Zam stared ahead at Hestia and Bonnyman who they were rapidly approaching and wondered if he could trust anyone at all, let alone a psychopathic ghost. And what was trust anyway, but a passing act of faith?

123

15

Bonnyman's wyrm was fast, but not as fast as Q, and Zam easily caught up with both Bonnyman and Hestia. As he flew alongside Bonnyman, the zombie leader of the Picts gazed across at him.

Zam smiled and waved.

'I'm just going to fly up ahead, to scout,' Zam shouted, 'let me know if you want me to slow down so you can keep up with me.'

Bonnyman turned away from him.

Using the joysticks to manoeuvre Q, Zam weaved a twisting path between Bonnyman and Hestia, then turned back and did the same thing again, smiling at Xara as he did.

'This is amazing,' Xara shouted as he passed by her.

'This is flying for real,' Zam hollered back in response, before speeding off in front of them once more. 'Come on, Q, let's see how fast you are capable of going.'

Q responded by launching into turbo-charge and Zam was forced back into Q's seat by the power of the thrust, as they left their companions behind like they weren't even moving.

'Grandfather's built you like a jet fighter,' Zam yelled.

'I'd be more like a rocket if I wasn't carrying you,' Q said.

Zam laughed. 'Yeah, but you wouldn't look half as good if you weren't carrying me.'

Where Mandrake Ackx's underworld sky beneath the streets of Newcastle was red and forever shifting, the Pict underworld sky was motionless and reflective. A deep blue, it was more like a perfectly calm ocean tipped upside down than the sky. And the air in the Pict underworld this high up smelled of the ocean. Zam wondered if that was something to do with the underworld or something to do with him. He eased back on Q's joysticks and waited for the others to catch up while he thought about Grandfather, wondering how he was coping looking after Xara's sister. And Xara, so much had happened to her these past few days, he wondered how she was keeping it all together. Maybe that was a ghost thing; maybe ghosts were able to keep their emotions in check better than humans. That didn't seem right, Xara in ghost form or Xara in human form, he was sure she would be the same as far as what she said or how she reacted to a situation. Her mind was the same; it was just her appearance that was different.

He guessed.

It would have been cool knowing her before she died. They would have been good friends if he knew her then, he was sure of that. What was she to him now? Still a friend, until she disappeared, until the light took her away. He would miss her when that happened. He didn't want to think about that happening, so he leant back in the seat and stared upwards, watching his reflection in the deep blue sky above.

***

Bonnyman stopped regularly to rest the wyrm, which seemed to have very low levels of energy. Zam was pleased he did, as it meant he could stretch and relieve the tension in his muscles. He asked Q how long his battery pack would last and Q reminded him that it was one of his Grandfather's inventions, a mix of underworld magic and man-made technology. It would either last forever or blow up as soon as it was switched on. Seeing as it didn't blow up when it was first used, Q said he guessed it would last indefinitely.

They drank water from streams Bonnyman guided them to, and ate vegetation from plants he told them were safe to eat. The water tasted stale and the plants tasted of nothing at all. Zam wasn't surprised the underworld appeared deserted. It looked and smelled beautiful, but it tasted unremarkable. As they started to settle down for the night, Bonnyman built a fire and, when it was blazing, he started to eat another kriung. While he ate, Zam and Xara left the camp. Zam didn't want to think about how the kriung tasted.

'Don't wander off too far,' Hestia told Zam. 'Stay within the light of the fire. The underworld comes alive at night time.'

When Bonnyman finished eating, he fed the remains of the kriung to the wyrm, which lay dozing, almost invisible just outside the ring of light coming from the fire. Zam didn't think the wyrm would get much sustenance from what remained of the kriung. He was sure it would need to eat more soon and didn't like the way it looked at him, as if he was a meal fit for a wyrm fed on kriung remains. The wyrm left camp shortly after eating and Bonnyman told him it was hunting for its own food in the night-time underworld skies.

'Can't you find something else to eat other than kriung?' Zam asked Bonnyman, as they settled down for the night around the camp fire.

The zombie looked as though he would not answer Zam. He stared into the heart of the fire thinking his own thoughts. 'When I first became a zombie,' he eventually said, 'my appetite could not be sated, no matter how much human flesh I ate. And I ate a lot of human flesh. I cannot eat dead flesh – it must be fresh off the bone. If I eat dead flesh, I vomit as soon as it hits my stomach and my skin bubbles up like there is a war raging beneath it. My appetite increases tenfold and I am uncontrollable then. I eat whatever human flesh I come upon no matter if it is friend or foe. Kriungs keep me almost human in nature.'

'What are these kriung creatures?' Xara asked. 'Where do they come from?'

'They are Mandrake Ackx's creation. A mutation he developed with a human scientist working for him. They are part bonobo ape, part human, and part underworld dwarf. They sustain me better than human flesh. Without them, I would need to eat a family of humans on a weekly basis. Mandrake made them docile, with no sense of pain. They do not feel anything when I eat them.'

'And that makes it right?' Xara said.

'In my world there is no right or wrong. There is simply existence and non-existence.'

'I think it would be better to not exist than to subsist the way you do.'

Zam stared across at Hestia, who had morphed back into the form of a woman, with long hair covering most of her body. 'Was the scientist who helped make the kriungs my grandfather, Hestia?

Hestia looked away and then back towards Zam. 'I do not know all of the experiments Eli worked on with my father.'

'But there is a chance it was Grandfather?'

'Yes, that is a possibility.'

'There is a lot I don't know about him.'

'It is the same with everyone, we all hide things from

each other. The world would be…uninteresting, if we knew everything about the people we share our life with.'

'Maybe we wouldn't share our lives with certain people if we knew certain things about them.'

'Precisely,' Hestia said.

'Why did Ackx bring the kriungs to life for you?' Zam said to Bonnyman.

'You ask too many questions,' Bonnyman said.

Zam stared Hestia's way. He could see she was in no mood to answer his question either.

'Ackx must have owed him big time,' Q said in his drawly Clint Eastwood voice. 'A favour like that doesn't come cheap.'

Bonnyman spat into the fire. 'A favour like that is only made between psychosis and a lust for power.'

Zam knew all about Ackx's lust for power, but he didn't think he'd witnessed a fraction of Bonnyman's psychosis.

***

Zam didn't sleep well that night. He dreamt about slaughterhouses in the underworld where kriungs were hung upside down by their feet on mechanical tracks that slowly transported them towards a circular blade perfectly aligned with their necks. As kriung heads were sliced off and rolled across the floor towards him, his dream transported him to an underworld burger house.

He sat alone in a cubicle with a burger held between his hands and when he took a bite out of it, he realised it wasn't a beef burger he was eating, it was a kriung burger.

It tasted delicious.

The next morning, Xara helped him with his leg stretches as Zam lay on the soft, blue grass covering the ground where Bonnyman had chosen as their camp for the night. She held her ghost hands beneath Zam's knee as he moved his leg backwards and forwards. Zam stared at Xara as she helped him. The look of concentration on her face made him wonder if that was why she was tingling where he touched her. He didn't want to ask her in case the tingling stopped.

'Why were you so restless last night?' Xara asked.

'I was dreaming.'

'What did you dream about?'

'Didn't you see what I was dreaming about?'

'I couldn't see last night. It was like your mind was inside a dark, misty night. Tell me what you were dreaming about.'

'I only want to tell you about the good dreams,' Zam said.

Xara tried to get him to tell her about the dream and when he wouldn't, she ignored him when he tried to talk to her and he realised then that girls were still like girls, even when they were ghosts.

As they continued their journey, Zam flew behind Hestia and Bonnyman, staring at the sack fastened to

Bonnyman's wyrm. There was no indication of movement inside the sack. He wondered what the kriungs were thinking, wondered if they thought at all or if they were simply mindless. He hoped they didn't think, he hoped they were mindless. He wanted the kriungs to be unaware of everything going on in their lives.

As the day passed and darkness began to descend in the underworld, Zam expected Bonnyman to land and make a camp for the night, but he didn't. They continued to fly until it was fully dark and the only thing to guide Zam in the blackness was Q's light reflecting off the back of Bonnyman's wyrm. It wasn't until Zam saw the lights in the distance that he realised they had arrived at the Wiccan coven. He stared at Xara and saw that she was watching him without giving away what she was feeling. Her face seemed to be getting paler. He wondered if that was a ghost thing, or maybe the effect of Q's light. He wondered then if she would start to grow younger like Slink had before he left Zam. And what would she do if they found the shadow wraith at the coven? He knew what he would do if the wraith had done the same thing to his parents. He guessed he would soon find out if Xara was capable of doing the same things he was capable of doing. The things that never ended the way he wanted them to end.

16

The coven was no more than a small settlement consisting of a dozen or so huts equally spaced around a stone building with two spires crookedly reaching for the sky. As they descended from the air, Zam saw that the structures had been arranged to form the shape of a pentagram, with the stone building in the centre and the largest of the huts forming the five points of the star. Bonnyman directed his wyrm to land outside the perimeter of the coven and as soon as Hestia landed and Xara dismounted, she morphed into the form of a small girl with long dark hair that reached down to her feet. Zam recognised the girl from his time in Mandrake Ackx's underworld.

'Why are you pretending to be a child?' Zam asked Hestia.

'I'm not pretending,' Hestia said. 'Haven't you ever heard the expression *you are only as young as you feel?*'

Bonnyman jumped from his wyrm and headed

straight for the entranceway of the main structure. The human-like inhabitants of the coven stood silently by and watched without making any attempt to stop or talk to him. When Q finished transforming back into a motorised wheelchair, Zam followed Bonnyman with Hestia and Xara walking at his side. As they stepped through the doorway, Zam saw that he had entered what appeared to be a church. Like Bonnyman's tent, the structure seemed much larger on the inside compared to how it appeared on the outside and Zam made a mental note to forget about space and dimensions when he was in the underworld. Simple wooden pews on either side of him were divided by a narrow aisle with an uneven stone floor. Wooden statues stood at the end of each pew with their heads bowed and their hands clasped in prayer. At the end of the aisle, Bonnyman stood in front of a seated statue of a half-man, half-goat. The top half of the statue consisted of a slim, yet muscular man with long, curly hair and curved horns on either side of his head, while the statue's woollen covered legs ended with cloven hooves instead of feet. When the statue stood up from its seated position, Zam realised it was not a statue at all but a living creature. It towered above Bonnyman, clearly angry.

The zombie appeared unfazed.

'You come unannounced,' the half-man, half-goat said, 'just like your last visit. I see you have still not learned the way of things.'

'This is my territory,' Bonnyman replied, 'and while

you are in my territory, I do not need to announce my coming.'

'This may be your territory,' the creature said in a soft, almost female-like voice, 'but that does not mean you have to be discourteous.'

As Zam stared at the creature, he saw a female ghost carrying a scythe twice her size materialise behind Bonnyman.

'What are you staring at?' Xara whispered.

Zam felt the familiar sensation of tiny icicles prickling his back after Xara whispered in his ear. He was almost lost in the effect. 'The ghost behind Bonnyman,' he managed to say.

'What ghost?' Xara asked.

The ghost stared at Zam. 'You can see me?' she asked in a surprised voice.

Zam nodded his head, realising that no one else could see the ghost.

'Nothing, it doesn't matter,' Zam whispered to Xara.

'Apologies,' Hestia said as she approached the creature. 'The nature of our business meant that we had to act with haste.'

The creature considered Hestia for a moment before speaking. 'The nature of your business is such that you cannot even find time for introductions?' it eventually said.

Hestia bowed her head. 'My name is Hestia,' she said, 'Lady of the Angles Underworld.' She turned towards

Zam. 'This is Napoleon Xylophone and his friend Xara.'

'And if you are interested, I'm Q,' Q said.

The creature stepped down from the altar and walked towards Zam. When it reached him it bent down and sniffed the top of his head. 'This is the child who defeated your father?' the creature said to Hestia.

'Yes,' Hestia replied.

'Curious,' the creature said.

'May I ask who you are?' Xara said to the creature.

The creature turned her attention to Xara. 'You may indeed, child. Some call me the Horned God, but you can call me Pan.'

'You are really a god?' Zam said.

Pan glared at Bonnyman. 'To some, yes.'

'Should I bow down in front of you?'

Pan laughed and it felt like music playing inside Zam's head. 'I am not your god, child. There is no need for you to bow down to me.'

'Enough,' Bonnyman said. 'We need to talk about a shadow wraith.'

Zam watched the zombie closely, wondering if it was because he hadn't eaten since the night before that he was so testy.

'What about a shadow wraith?' Pan said.

'We are looking for a wraith with only one arm,' Zam said and despite the circumstances, he couldn't help but smile.

'There is no such wraith here.'

'Are you sure?' Bonnyman said.

'Yes, I'm sure. I think I would know if there was a wraith with only one arm in my coven.'

Zam felt something stir in his pocket. 'The wraith's finger is moving,' he said.

Bonnyman smiled. 'Put it on the altar. Let's see which direction it crawls towards.'

Zam pulled the wraith's finger from his pocket and placed it on the altar. At first it did not move. After a moment, it turned itself around and started to move towards the right of the altar. Bonnyman stared in the direction the finger moved. Zam followed his gaze and saw a door directly across from the altar where the finger was heading. Bonnyman picked up the finger, raced over to the door and opened it. Looking past the zombie, Zam could see the door led to a small antechamber. Bonnyman entered the chamber and looked around. There were three other doors apart from the one he entered. He placed the finger on the floor and it started to crawl like an inch worm to the door on Bonnyman's left. Bonnyman entered the door and disappeared from view. A moment later, Zam heard a noise above and when he looked up, he saw the wraith's head appear over the side of a narrow balcony.

Bonnyman had his hands around the wraith's neck, choking it mercilessly.

'Don't kill it,' Hestia shouted, 'we need to know what it knows.'

Bonnyman looked down at Hestia and, for a moment, Zam thought he was going to ignore her, but he loosened his grip on the wraith and pulled it away from the edge of the balcony. As soon as he did, the wraith slipped from his grasp and jumped over the balcony. Moving rapidly, it seemed to glide across the space as it headed to the rear of the church away from them.

Hestia was the first to react, morphing into an incredibly ugly spider the size of a bear. As she transformed, she spat a silk web at the wraith and it tumbled to the floor with the web wrapped around its legs. The wraith struggled against the silk strands and the more it struggled, the tighter the web entwined around it.

'Do something to stop it spinning away like it did in Xara's house,' Zam shouted at Hestia, thinking it still wasn't over.

'Do not worry.' Hestia said. 'It can only whirl-shift in your domain, not the underworld.'

Bonnyman bounded out of the antechamber and ran towards the wraith. When he reached it, he grabbed hold of it by its hair and roughly dragged it across the floor. Part of the web came away from the wraith as Bonnyman made his way towards the others and dumped the wraith on the flat, stone surface of the altar. Zam noticed for the first time that it still only had one arm. It must not have been in the coven long enough to get its arm replaced in whatever way the Wiccan witches did such things.

'I thought you said this wraith wasn't in your coven,' Bonnyman glared at Pan.

The ghost moved behind Bonnyman and raised the scythe. 'Pan did not know,' she said to Zam in a thick Scottish accent.

'It is true, he didn't know,' he heard another voice say.

The voice came from no one Zam could see.

'My mother's name is Eufame,' the voice added. *'Isn't that a beautiful name?'*

Zam stared at the ghost behind Bonnyman and suddenly knew where the voice came from.

'Well?' Bonnyman said to Pan.

Pan stared at the wraith without speaking.

'Pan did not know,' Zam said.

Bonnyman turned towards Zam. 'What? How do you know that?'

'Eufame told me.'

Pan raised his head and stared at Zam.

'Who is Eufame?' Bonnyman asked.

'The ghost standing behind you. The one who looks like she is waiting to slice you in half if you attempt to harm her god.'

Bonnyman stared at Zam for a brief moment that seemed much longer. 'How do you know you can trust what this ghost says?' he asked without turning around to see if the ghost really was behind him.

'Because her baby said exactly the same thing. I'm sure her baby doesn't know how to lie.'

As soon as the words left Zam's mouth, the ghost behind Bonnyman became visible to everyone.

'My baby?' the ghost said. 'You heard Freya speak?'

'Yes, she thinks your name is beautiful.'

'You seem to have forgotten we have a wraith to interrogate here,' Bonnyman said to Zam. 'Leave the ghost talk for later.'

'I need to know about Freya,' Eufame said to Zam.

Zam held out an outstretched hand to the ghost. 'We can talk later, let's deal with this wraith first.'

Eufame looked like she was about to race over to Zam, but she seemed to change her mind and continued to hold the scythe prone next to Bonnyman.

Xara walked across to the altar, standing next to Eufame. 'You killed my parents,' she said to the wraith.

'I killed you too,' the wraith replied.

Bonnyman squeezed harder on the wraith's neck. 'Don't disrespect my companions.'

The wraith began to choke as Bonnyman's grip tightened.

Hestia changed back into the little girl and stood beside Bonnyman. She gently placed her hand on top of his. 'We need to keep her alive, Isaac. We need to know what she knows.'

Bonnyman eased his grip on the wraith. 'Who sent you to kill the boy?'

The wraith began to cough and Bonnyman waited patiently for it to be able to talk again.

'I can't tell you anything,' the wraith eventually managed to say. 'I'd be dead as soon as I did.'

'You are already dead,' Bonnyman said, 'you just don't realise it yet.'

'Then kill me now and get it over with.'

'There are different ways to die. Nice ways and not so nice ways.'

'Kill me any way you like, none of your ways are as bad as the ways of the…'

'Of who?'

'I told you, I cannot say.'

'Your loyalty lies with me.'

'Me, be loyal to you?' the wraith laughed. 'You didn't even know I existed until today.'

'I am your leader.'

'In name only. You do nothing for me or anyone else but yourself.'

Bonnyman threw the wraith to the floor. 'We are not going to get anything from this thing.'

'There are truth serums we could use,' Pan said.

'You have them here?'

'Of course, this is a Wiccan coven.'

Zam stared at Xara, who in turn was watching the wraith intently. He could only imagine the pain she must have been feeling inside, thinking about her parents, her sister and what the wraith had done to them. He wished he could do something to ease her pain.

'Do it,' Bonnyman said to Pan.

Pan clapped his hands twice and as he did, the wooden statue at the end of the front row pew got up and walked towards them. The instant Zam turned around to stare at the statue, the wraith got up and made a dash towards him. It held a needle-like weapon in its one remaining hand.

Xara had not taken her eyes off the wraith since it first appeared and as soon as it moved, she grabbed the ghost scythe off Eufame, stepped forward and without any hesitation she sliced the wraith's head off.

'For my parents,' she said as the wraith's head landed on the floor and rolled a couple of times before coming to settle against one of Q's wheels.

Bonnyman quickly walked over to the head and picked it up by the hair. He held it in front of his face. 'Tell me whose orders you follow,' he said in a gentle voice that Zam didn't think he possessed.

The wraith looked past Bonnyman, staring at its body twitching on the floor. 'Never your orders,' it gasped, before closing its eyes forever.

Pan walked across to Zam, placing his hand on his shoulder. 'How did you see Eufame?' he asked.

'I'm not sure,' Zam said.

'There is much about him still to be learned,' Hestia said.

Pan and Hestia stared at each other and Zam got the impression there was much more going on in the look they shared than simply the gaze. He turned his attention to Xara. She still held onto the scythe and stared at the wraith's head, which Bonnyman had placed on the altar.

'Xara, are you alright?' he asked.

'What do you think?' she said, continuing to stare at the wraith's head.

'Bravo, girl,' Bonnyman said, 'now we have nothing but a dead end.'

Xara glared at Bonnyman. 'That thing killed my parents. Believe me, now that it is gone I have much more than a dead end to hold onto.'

Eufame placed her hand on Xara's shoulder and took

the scythe away from her. 'You saved your friend's life, child. You did well.'

Xara pulled away from Eufame, sat down on the step leading up to the altar and started to weep. Zam wanted to sit with her, to comfort her in some way, but Eufame stood in front of him.

'Tell me about my baby,' she said.

Zam listened to Xara weep. He didn't know what to do. He closed his eyes and said *Xyz*, over and over in his mind.

Freya started to speak to him.

'Mother needs to leave this place. She needs to transcend.'

'Freya wants you to cross over,' Zam said, opening his eyes and seeing Eufame still standing in front of him.

Eufame looked horrified. 'No, I can never do that.'

'Why not?'

'To do so would destroy Freya.'

'How do you know that?'

'I can't communicate with her, but I can feel her, inside me. I have always felt her. If I cross over, I'm afraid that she will be no more than a thought inside my mind.'

Zam didn't know how to answer that and Freya remained silent. 'Why is it only I could see you before?' he asked, without knowing what else to ask.

'I keep myself hidden from everyone; I don't know why you could see me.'

'How do you keep hidden?'

'I think myself invisible and so I am.'

'I wish I could do that, especially when my grandfather is looking for me to polish his shoes.'

'Have you ever tried to think yourself invisible?'

'Only when Grandfather is looking for me to polish his shoes. It never works, though, he always finds me.'

Eufame smiled and it made Zam feel good that he could make a ghost smile. He looked across at Xara and saw that she had stopped weeping. She seemed to be listening to his conversation with Eufame. He remembered how she had looked both magnificent and scary at the same time when she sliced off the wraith's head. He thought about the butcher ghost, how the meat cleaver it carried cut into the night gaunts, but passed straight through Zam when the ghost had tried to cut him at school. He wondered if the cleaver would still pass through his flesh if the butcher ghost used it on him in the underworld.

'How did Xara managed to slice off the wraith's head?' he asked Eufame. 'The scythe you have hold of looks as much a ghost as you do?'

'This is the underworld. What you know and believe of your world, does not necessarily apply here.'

'That's all you can say about it?'

'That is all I can say,' Eufame said.

Bonnyman faced Pan. 'You would have had your assassin ghost slice me in half?' he said.

'If I had known she was there and you tried to do

144

something I didn't like, yes. But I did not know she was present. She was invisible to me like she was to everyone else except for your young companion, Napoleon.'

Bonnyman looked unconvinced.

'Call me Zam, please, Pan.'

'If you were disrespectful to a god I follow,' Eufame said to Bonnyman. 'I would protect him…'

'With your life,' Bonnyman said before Eufame could continue. 'Guess what, you are already dead.'

'As are you,' Eufame said.

'How long have you been here, Eufame?' Pan asked.

'Not long.'

'Why didn't you make your presence known?'

'I'm not good in crowds.'

'Why not?' Zam asked.

'It's a long story and I don't want to think about it.'

'Okay.'

'You have beautiful hair,' Xara said, staring at Eufame.

'Thank you.'

'Who are you?' Hestia asked.

'In another life, I was known as Eufame Maclerie.'

Xara moved closer to Eufame. 'Zam said you have a child.'

Eufame held onto her stomach. 'Yes,'

'You are pregnant?' Q said.

'She was pregnant when she was murdered,' Hestia said, 'during the witch hunts in the 1800's. Her lover tried to save her, but the mob wanted blood that day and he was forcibly restrained. He had to watch as she burned at the stake.'

Xara closed her eyes with her hand on her brow. 'They killed you when you were pregnant?'

'Such things are not uncommon throughout human history,' Bonnyman said.

'You were human once,' Zam said.

Bonnyman smiled, revealing broken, yellowed teeth.

'You've been a ghost for over 200 years...' Xara quickly said. 'What have you been doing in all that time?'

'Wandering the City of the Dead below Edinburgh, mostly. Recently, I was drawn here, to the coven. I'm not sure why.'

'Maybe it had something to do with Napoleon,' Hestia said.

'What do you mean?' Zam asked.

'You are much more than simply clairvoyant. I have never seen anyone take to the gift as quickly as you. Not only do you see the spirit world, you have an instinctive understanding of spirits and their needs. They are drawn towards you like no one else I know.'

'*Will you go back to the City of the Dead, Zam,*' Freya said, '*to help the children?*'

'What children?'

'My daughter is speaking to you again?' Eufame said.

'She asked me to go back to the City of the Dead, to help the children.'

'*The children behind the wall, they are so sad.*'

'She wants me to help the children behind the wall. Who are they?'

'I don't know,' Eufame said. 'Would you ask my daughter to speak to me?'

'It is not possible for her to hear me. I can hear her, though. I like it when she speaks to me.'

'She said she can hear you speak, Eufame, but it is not possible for her to speak to you.'

Eufame looked disappointed.

'She also said that she loves it when you speak to her.'

'Thank you,' Eufame said.

Zam turned towards Hestia. 'What do we do now? Should we go to the City of the Dead to help these children?'

'The threat to your life has not gone away,' Hestia said. 'We do not know if there are others hunting you apart from the doppelganger and the wraith. You are safer here than in your own world. Perhaps we should follow the path your spirit friend has laid out for you and see where it takes us. What do you think, Isaac?'

Bonnyman grunted. 'Now the wraith is dead, we have no way of learning who is behind the threat to the boy's life. If another attempt is made to kill him, who better than you or I to protect him? He should stay here until we get a better understanding of what we are dealing with.'

Eufame turned towards Hestia. 'A doppelganger attacked him?'

147

'Yes,' Hestia said, 'it tried to absorb him.'

'You could track it down through a mirror's edge.'

'You don't track down a doppelganger. It exists in illusion. A doppelganger is only seen when it wants to be seen.'

'If it wants Zam, then it would show itself to him.'

'Yes, that is true, but the risk of it absorbing him is too high. Napoleon was fortunate the last time he fought Krackle. He may not be so fortunate next time. And we would not be able to help – Krackle would not appear if we were with Napoleon.'

'What is mirror's edge?' Zam said.

'It's a gateway into a mirror,' Eufame replied.

'I can get inside a mirror? Cool.'

'Not so cool if there is also a doppelganger inside the mirror,' Hestia said.

'Please help the children.'

Zam stared at Eufame. 'I'm not sure what I can do for the children in the City of the Dead, but your daughter seems to think I can help them. Until we know any better, I think we should return to Edinburgh and at least try to find the children.'

Xara walked towards the exit. 'I'm all for helping someone,' she said. 'It will make a change from killing someone.'

At the exit to the church, Xara didn't bother trying to open the door, she walked straight through it. Zam pushed forwards on Q's controls and raced after her, hoping she wasn't about to lose her ghost-mind after all the badness she had witnessed these past few days. Hoping too, that she wouldn't disappear like the butcher ghost into that place he went where Zam could not follow.

18

They stayed at the Wiccan coven that night and rose early the next morning with the intention of returning to Bonnyman's camp before heading to The City of the Dead. Before they left, Pan took Zam to one side and told him he would always be welcomed by the Wicca, wherever he may find them.

'Why would I be welcome?' Zam asked.

'You will make a good leader,' Pan said. 'Trust your instincts, child.'

A little confused, Zam thanked the Horned God and joined the others as they readied themselves for the journey. Eufame rode with Xara on the back of Hestia, who had once more morphed into a wyrm. As they made their way back to Bonnyman's camp, Zam noticed that the underworld sky was no longer reflective or blue. It was grey and flat.

'What's wrong with the sky?' Zam asked Hestia, the first night they rested.

'It must be Isaac,' Hestia replied. 'The sky reflects the mood of the most powerful being in the underworld.'

Zam looked across at Bonnyman as he collected firewood. 'He doesn't look any different to the other day when the sky was blue.'

'Who knows the workings of a zombie's mind?' Hestia said.

Zam thought about Hestia's words. 'Is Bonnyman really more powerful than you?'

'He is the leader of the Picts. This is his realm. In the underworld, every blade of grass, mouthful of air and drop of water is connected to the leader. The land and the leader have a special bond. The land protects its leader.'

'Is the leader stronger than a god like Pan?'

'It depends upon what you mean by stronger.'

'Could Pan beat Bonnyman in a fight?'

'I do not know.'

'Why isn't Pan the leader of the Pict underworld?'

'A god cannot lead underworld creatures. A god can only inspire followers.'

'What makes Pan a god?'

'His followers, without followers he is nothing.'

'If he didn't have any followers he wouldn't exist?'

'In a way.'

'What kind of way?'

'He would exist as part of the world like the breeze does or a rain shower. He wouldn't exist as the being you saw in the coven.'

151

'Why? Who makes up all these rules?'

'There are no rules, there is merely evolution.'

'I think you could beat Bonnyman in a fight. In your underworld realm or his, I think you could beat him.'

'Why would I want to fight Isaac?'

'I don't know. I just want to know where we stand if it came down to a fight with him. I don't trust him.'

'Why do you say that?'

'I don't like the way he looks at people.'

'He is a zombie, he looks at everyone the same way.'

'It's not just the part where he looks like he wants to eat everyone.'

'What then?'

'It's when he looks like he wants to be your friend that I don't trust him.'

'He's not as bad as you think.'

'He eats kriungs when they are still alive.'

'It is part of his nature. He does a fine job of fighting against his nature.'

'Why does he fight his nature?'

'Because he wants to be human again.'

'You wouldn't think so. Not the way he talks about humans.'

Bonnyman returned to the camp and placed some of the wood he had collected on the fire. Sitting down beside the fire, he opened the sack which had the last kriung inside. Zam turned away, ready to make his way over to Xara and Eufame, who were talking by the river.

'I don't have much choice in the way of meat,' Bonnyman said to Zam. 'I can offer you some of this kriung if you like.'

Zam turned Q around and faced Bonnyman.

'I can roast it for you, if you prefer,' Bonnyman said before Zam could speak.

Zam couldn't decide if Bonnyman was mocking him or not. 'I think I'll give roasted kriung a miss,' he said.

'My appetite is not what it was either,' Bonnyman said, tossing the sack to one side. 'I think I will also give kriung a miss tonight.'

Zam approached the fire and stopped opposite Bonnyman. 'How did you become leader of the Pict underworld?' he asked, wondering for the first time how a zombie could be the ruler of an underworld realm.

'I ate the previous leader. A lesson needed to be taught.'

'That would do it. Did he taste any good?'

'No, he tasted exactly like you would expect a swamp grizzard to taste.'

'I'm pretty sure I'd taste worse than a swamp grizzard.'

Bonnyman poked the fire with a stick he was holding. 'You don't want to know how I think you would taste, or how much I want to eat you.'

'I think I already know. I've seen the way you stare at me and Hestia.'

Bonnyman continued to prod the fire without speaking.

'How did you become a zombie?' Zam asked.

'I ate a dead changeling.'

Zam looked at Hestia and then back at Bonnyman. 'Why did you do that?'

'Sometimes the choice is not always your own.'

'Now you sound like a changeling. Maybe it has something to do with something you ate.'

'And you always sound like a swamp grizzard, Napoleon,' Hestia said.

Zam was about to ask Hestia what a swamp grizzard actually was, but changed his mind. 'What's it like being a zombie?' he asked Bonnyman instead.

'Lonely.'

'Why don't you start a zombie apocalypse, then you'd have loads of zombie friends?'

'No one would thank me for turning them into a zombie.'

'Could you turn me into a zombie by biting me?'

'No.'

'How then?'

'By forcing you to eat changeling flesh.'

'Can we talk about something else other than eating changelings?' Hestia said.

'Have you ever tried just eating vegetables?' Zam said.

'Not eating meat makes me angry. You wouldn't want to see me when I'm angry.'

'Now you sound like the Hulk,' Q said.

Bonnyman frowned. 'Who is the Hulk?'

'Don't listen to Q,' Zam said. 'The Hulk is a fictional character, he isn't real.'

'How do you know the Hulk isn't real?' Q said. 'You used to think zombies weren't real.'

'Have you ever wanted to be human again?' Xara asked Bonnyman.

Zam turned around and saw Xara and Eufame standing behind him. He hadn't realised they had joined them.

'Every day I think about being human. I would give anything to become a man again.'

Zam picked up a stick by his feet and started to poke the fire with it. 'Isn't there some supernatural way of turning yourself back into a man?'

'No,' Bonnyman said, 'I am lost forever. There is no way to bring a dead thing back to life.'

'So you will live forever as a zombie? You will never die again?'

'This is not exactly living; I am more dead than alive. But yes, it seems that I will remain this way forever. I do not age. My wounds heal quickly, like I was never wounded before and all I need to survive is live flesh.'

'What if there was no living flesh for you to eat?'

'Like I said, it would make me angry. I do not know if I would die again, though.'

'All supernatural creatures must eventually succumb to lunacy; it is the natural order of things,' Hestia said. 'No creature can live forever without the mind yielding.'

155

'Are you afraid of going crazy, Hestia?' Bonnyman asked.

'I am afraid of what I might do once it happens.'

'Is that what happened to your father?' Zam asked.

'No, my father was born crazy.'

'Is there anything you can do to stop it happening to you?' Zam asked.

'I will eventually lose my mind as surely as all humans will eventually do something bad.'

'What will happen to you then?'

'Hopefully, someone will be kind enough chop off my head,' Hestia said, looking at Xara.

'I could never do that,' Xara said.

Hestia laughed. 'Do not worry child, I would never ask you to do that.'

Zam had a thought. 'The underworld seems an empty place. There aren't many creatures living here.'

'It is true, there are not as many here as there used to be,' Bonnyman said. 'The creatures of the underworld are a dying breed.'

'They are dying?' Zam said.

'Yes,' Hestia replied. 'It has been this way for two thousand years.'

'Why are they dying?' Xara asked.

Bonnyman snapped the stick he had hold of and threw it onto the fire. 'Because they can no longer reproduce – they are sterile.'

'You can't have any children?'

'Not since the crucifixion,' Hestia said.

'God has stopped you reproducing?'

'Supernatural creatures that breed with humans can still reproduce,' Bonnyman said. 'It seems that God has a perverse sense of humour.'

'It is difficult to know the reason for the changes in the underworld,' Hestia said.

'God never gave any reasons in the past,' Bonnyman said, 'now that he has stopped speaking, there is even less chance of finding out a reason.'

'God has stopped speaking to Time too.' Zam said.

'How could you know that?' Bonnyman asked.

'Time told me that God does not speak anymore.'

Bonnyman looked as though he was going to press Zam further, but Hestia spoke before he could.

'It is true, Napoleon has spoken to Time. My father and Zam's grandfather created something which allowed him to do so.'

Mandrake Ackx hadn't developed the Relater so that he could simply speak to Time, Zam thought. He had developed it so that he could become Time. Zam stopped him from doing it and almost killed Ackx in the process.

'Why has God stopped speaking to everyone?' Xara said.

'Maybe He is bored with everyone,' Q said. 'I can see why He would become bored.'

Bonnyman stared at Hestia. 'How old are you?' he asked.

Hestia sat down by the fire. 'Old enough to know better than to tell you my age.'

'Were you alive when God talked to the creatures of the underworld?' Bonnyman continued.

'Yes.'

'Did He ever talk to you?'

'Yes.'

'What did He say?'

'He told me to never stop listening and He would never stop speaking.'

'But He did stop.'

'I'm not sure He did,' Hestia sighed. 'I think it might be the rest of us who have stopped listening in the way He wants us to listen.'

'How does he want us to listen?' Zam asked.

'That's a question you need to ask Him,' Hestia replied.

When they reached Bonnyman's camp, the zombie leader of the Pict Underworld quickly dismounted his wyrm and raced into the tent. Zam didn't need to enter the tent to know what he would be doing inside and he didn't want to enter the tent for that same reason. He stared at the gaunts, who paced the opening to the tent eyeing him warily. When they crouched down with the hairs on their backs raised and started to snarl, Zam told Q to arm his weapon systems and prepare to blast them out of the underworld.

'What is it with you and those creatures?' Hestia asked.

'I don't think they like his wheelchair,' Q said.

'It isn't anything to do with Zam,' Eufame said. 'It's the ghost behind us they are wary about.'

Zam turned around and stared through the gaps in the trees. At first, he couldn't make anything out – then he saw the butcher ghost walking towards them.

He smiled.

'You know him?' Eufame asked Zam.

'I thought I knew him. I thought he was a psychopath. Now I'm not so sure.'

When the butcher ghost reached them, he stood next to Zam and wordlessly stared at the night gaunts.

'It's good to have you back,' Zam said.

The butcher ghost remained silent and unmoving.

'The way these guys are staring at each other, I think they must be in love,' Q said.

Zam studied the butcher ghost, pleased to see he looked uninjured. The wounds the gaunts had inflicted on him were no longer visible and if he was hurt during the fall from Q, no evidence of it remained.

'*It makes me want to weep.*'

'What does?' Zam asked Freya.

'*Feeling the things your friend has gone through when he was alive.*'

'What kind of things?'

'Is Freya talking to you again?' Eufame asked.

'Yes,' Zam replied

'*Bad things.*'

Eufame stepped closer to Zam. 'What is she saying?'

'*Things he can't forget. He is a bad man, he has done many bad things when he was alive and also as a ghost.*'

'She's talking about the ghost standing next to me.'

'*He wasn't always bad, something happened to change him that he keeps shrouded. It feels like it involved family.*'

Zam looked at Xara, but asked Freya the question. 'Can you see past the shroud?'

Freya didn't answer at first. Instead, she began to weep. When she finally spoke, Zam didn't want to hear what she had to say.

'He will always be bad.'

'What happened to him?' Xara asked.

'She doesn't know,' Zam said, suddenly feeling weary. His muscles ached like they were not a part of him, like they wanted him to suffer. He unbuckled the strap and lifted himself out of Q. Lying on the ground, he started his leg stretches and tried not to think about bad things.

Xara joined him on the floor and supported his legs while he stretched. She had quickly learned how to help him with his exercises. Zam felt disappointed that he couldn't feel any tingling when she touched him, like he usually could. He wondered then if the tingling wasn't real, if it was all in his mind. He closed his eyes and tried not to think about anything.

Bonnyman exited the tent a short while later and left with the gaunts following him. He didn't say what he was doing or where he was going. Zam and the others settled beneath the trees opposite the tent and while eating some of the provisions the Wicca had given them, Zam wondered who the children were that Freya wanted him to help and how exactly he was supposed to help them. He also thought about Xara and her family. He hoped she wouldn't turn bad. Since she had beheaded the wraith, she had become distant and hardly talked to him. He didn't want her to become another butcher ghost. At the same time, he didn't know how to stop her becoming one. The butcher ghost remained standing, staring in the direction where Bonnyman and the gaunts had gone. Zam didn't want to know what was going through the butcher ghost's head; he didn't want to know that at all. Bonnyman returned alone a few hours later, saying nothing about where he had been or what he had done.

'I see your friend has returned,' Bonnyman said to Zam. 'He still does not like me.'

'He still doesn't like anyone,' Zam said.

'That's where you are wrong, he likes you.'

'It's a ghost thing,' Hestia said, 'all ghosts seem to like Napoleon.'

'I'd like him too, if I was a ghost,' Q said.

'I think it's time we went searching for Freya's children,' Zam said, dragging himself over to Q and pulling himself into his seat.

After they packed up their things, Bonnyman led them back to the place where they first entered his underworld. Xara walked over to the knoll at their right and as soon as her hand touched it, the ghost door appeared. She opened the ghost door and they followed her back into the City of the Dead below Edinburgh. The transition from the underworld air to the musty air that permeated the streets below Edinburgh was a shock to Zam and he started to cough almost as soon as he entered. He didn't stop until Hestia handed him a water canister and he took a drink from it.

'The air in the world of men is polluted even in the places where they no longer live,' Bonnyman said.

Zam didn't rise to Bonnyman's baiting. 'Where are the children?' he asked Freya after drinking the water.

'They are behind the wall.'

'Which wall?'

The others stood silently watching Zam as he continued to talk to Eufame's daughter.

'The wall the bad men built.'

Zam stared at Hestia. 'She said the children are behind a wall the bad men built.'

'I don't know where she means,' Hestia said.

'I think I know where she means,' Bonnyman said. 'During the dark days, a school was bricked up when the men who ran the city thought one of the children inside was infected with the plague. All of the children were forced to remain inside the school when they bricked it up. Some of their parents remained inside with them too.'

'That's so wrong,' Xara said.

'That is so like man,' Bonnyman said.

'Do you know where the school is located?' Zam asked.

'I have a rough idea,' Bonnyman replied.

'Lead the way then.'

Bonnyman didn't move at first. After a short while he stepped forwards and then quickly made his way down

163

the narrow street up ahead. He turned first left, then right, and without looking back to see if the others were following, he removed a metal lattice from a small opening and disappeared inside.

'I don't think he likes being told what to do,' Xara said to Zam as they tried to keep up with Bonnyman.

'I don't think he likes me telling him what to do,' Zam replied, pleased Xara was talking to him again.

Staring at the opening, Zam saw that Q would not be able to move in the cramped space and uneven floor in the form of a wheelchair and he asked him to change into the exoskeleton.

'I love being this way,' Q said a moment later after he had changed. 'I almost feel like a ghost in this form.'

'A ghost?' Zam said.

'Okay, I know I'm not exactly a ghost, but at least I'm ghost shaped.'

The small opening eventually led into a network of streets similar in construction to the ones they had just left. With no illumination in this part of the city, they were guided by Q's lights, which revealed how much dust hung in the air. Continuing to follow Bonnyman, it was some time later that he finally stopped. 'This is as far as I can take you,' he said to Hestia rather than Zam. 'I know the school is around here somewhere, but I don't know the exact location.'

'Can you help, Q?' Zam asked.

'I have nothing in my memory banks other than a simple map showing the main streets below the city.

There is no mention of a school anywhere on the map. Our current location is not detailed on it either.'

'What about your scanners?'

'They only have a short range; unless we are right on top of the school I won't be able to locate it.'

'Looks like I need to ask Grandfather to upgrade your scanners.'

'Can you ask him to upgrade my looks instead?'

'Your looks?'

'Yeah, I'd like to look like Ghost Rider rather than me.'

'You look fine as you are, Q.'

'That's easy for you to say.'

'What do you mean?'

'You have blue hair. I can never have blue hair.'

'It wouldn't suit you.'

'I know. That's why I want to go for a human skull look, like Ghost Rider with flames coming out of my eyes.'

'I don't think that look would suit you either.'

'What then?'

'I don't know, maybe something simple like chrome trim around your wheels.'

'That's all you see me as, a pair of wheels?'

'If you two are finished,' Bonnyman said, 'I have more important things to do.'

'Don't mind me,' Q said. 'I'm just a pair of wheels.'

Zam wanted to tell Q that he was more than a pair of wheels, but thought better of it. 'Do you know where the children are?' he asked Freya instead.

'We are close, I can feel them breathing.'

'How close?'

'The children are behind the wall.'

'Which wall?'

There was a pause before Freya answered.

'I do not know.'

Zam turned towards Xara and Eufame, who always seemed to be close together since they left the Wiccan coven. 'Can you scout around to see if you can locate the school? I mean, can you walk through a few walls to see if they lead into something we cannot see?'

'I can try,' Eufame said.

'Me too,' Xara added.

'Thanks,' Zam said. He turned towards the butcher ghost. 'How about you?'

The butcher ghost ignored him.

Xara and Eufame left them, with Xara walking through the wall to their left and Eufame walking through the wall to their right.

Xara returned a moment later. 'It's no use,' she said. 'I can't see anything, it's pitch black everywhere.'

'Can't you see in the dark?' Zam asked.

'I'm a ghost, not a bat,' Xara said.

Eufame returned a short while afterwards saying she also could not find the school.

'This is nonsense,' Bonnyman said. 'We are wasting our time here.'

'What do you suggest?' Zam said.

Before Bonnyman could answer, the butcher ghost walked past him, heading for an alleyway to their right.

'Where are you going?' Zam said.

The butcher ghost did not answer. It continued to walk up ahead. Zam followed and the others followed Zam. Three streets further on, the butcher ghost stopped at a dead end.

'What is it?' Zam asked. 'Is the school behind the wall?'

The butcher ghost stared back at Zam without saying anything, then moved away from the wall and leant against the adjacent wall with its arms and legs crossed, while still holding onto the meat cleaver.

Zam studied the wall. He could see that some of the bricks were slightly darker and a different texture to others. He swivelled Q's headlight and saw that the different coloured bricks formed what looked like the outline of an entranceway.

'There is a small room behind the wall,' Q said.

Xara moved next to the wall and bent into it so that her upper body disappeared into the bricks. She reappeared a moment later. 'There's something there, I can feel a presence, more than one presence. It's too dark for me to see anything. I can't be sure.'

'We need to find a way to get behind the wall,' Zam said.

'Stand clear,' Q said, as he backed away from the wall.

Once everyone had moved away, a red dot appeared

on the wall and as it moved in a straight line, the bricks it passed over began to smoulder. A moment later, part of the wall crumbled into pieces and dust plumed out. As the dust began to clear, Q's headlights revealed an opening. Bonnyman hurriedly pushed his way past Zam and began to move loose bricks from wall and the floor. When he had finished clearing a pathway, they followed Bonnyman into the opening and found that it led into a low ceilinged corridor. At the end of the corridor they found themselves in an antechamber with three further doorways. Bonnyman began to recite a rhyme while pointing at each door in turn: 'Eannie, meanie, miny mo, catch a changeling by the toe. If it screams, bite it off, eannie, meanie miny mo. The door on the left it is then.'

'I'm beginning to worry about you, Isaac,' Hestia said.

Bonnyman replied with a smile that made Zam worry about him too.

The zombie walked over to the door and twisted the handle, pushing it inwards as he did. The room behind the door was bare, except for a row of bunk beds positioned along the length of the wall opposite from where they now stood. Zam quickly scanned the room, seeing nothing of interest. Bonnyman walked across to the door opposite and opened it. Zam and the others followed and found themselves in an office similar in size to the antechamber. It too had three doorways and a large desk in the middle of the room. An upturned chair lay discarded behind the desk. Zam went over to the desk and opened the drawers. There was nothing inside them other than dust.

'This place doesn't look like a school,' Xara said.

'Schools in the time of the plague were different to the schools you know today,' Bonnyman said. 'And this place looks like it has been used for something else since it was a school.'

'How did the butcher know it would be here?' Zam asked Hestia.

'Haven't you noticed yet how ghosts have different abilities, Napoleon? Just like people have different levels of aptitudes and emotions, so are ghosts the same. It may seem unlikely, but witnessing what your friend has just done, I think he is an empath.'

'An empath, what's an empath?'

'Someone who is sensitive and finely tuned into the environment around them. They feel everything to the extreme. Empaths usually have big hearts; they are naturally generous and helpful to others. Your friend doesn't come across that way, I know, but it's the only explanation to how he found this place. I fear something bad must have happened in his life for him to be the way he is now.'

Zam thought about Freya's words when she tried to describe the butcher ghost.

'He will always be bad.'

Zam hoped Freya was wrong.

Bonnyman stepped past Zam. 'If you are finished

chattering,' he said, opening the door to the right, 'maybe we can move on.'

The door led back into the antechamber. Bonnyman strode over to the third door and pushed it open. He stood there for a moment without moving, staring into the room. When he turned around to face them, Zam was shocked to see a look of horror on his face. Bonnyman stepped back from the doorway and Zam shone Q's lights into the room. The light revealed five children sitting huddled together inside a cage in the corner of the room. He could see they were ghosts, but it took him a moment later to realise they were the ghosts of zombies.

The children did not move, even after Zam and the others entered the room. Each of them stared intently at the ground, like the ground was a movie screen showing the latest hot film. There were two boys and three girls and, despite their translucent features, they looked the same as Bonnyman, with pallid skin and dark, sunken eyes. As Q's lights illuminated more of the space, Zam saw an operating table in the centre of the room and a blank-walled structure in the opposite corner that could be no more than a holding cell of some kind.

'Help them Zam.'

'What am I supposed to do? I don't know how to help them.'

'Talk to them.'

'What do I say?'

Freya didn't answer.

170

'Q, please morph back into a wheelchair.'

'It's done,' Q said as Zam listened to the sound of Q changing shape and felt the exoskeleton shift around him.

When the noise stopped and Q was his usual shape, Zam wheeled himself over to the cage. Staring into it, he saw that the ghost children formed a circle around a heap of skeletons. Judging by their small size, Zam guessed the skeletons were once the ghost children who now surrounded them.

'Hi,' he said, 'I'm Zam.'

The ghost children did not respond. He grabbed hold of the iron railed door, attempting to open it and saw that the door had been padlocked shut. 'Q, can you do anything about this padlock?'

A metallic arm shot out from Q's side and as it headed towards the padlock, a thin metal strip extended from the arm and entered the padlock's key hole. The metal strip twisted a number of times in different directions before the padlock eventually sprung open. Zam removed the padlock from the hasp and opened the door to the cage.

'You stay here Q,' Zam said, as he slid out of Q's seat and shuffled into the cage, coming to a rest in-between the two ghost children nearest the doorway. The children remained motionless and Zam stared at the skeletons in front of him. The skeletons were dressed in ragged clothes and it looked like they were hugging each other in a final show of affection before death took them away.

'What happened?' Zam asked.

The ghost children remained perfectly still.

'It looks like you are good friends. Like you look out for each other. I wish I had friends who looked out for me when I'm at school. Or friends who would sit with me at lunch time. I usually have to sit alone.' Zam thought about Ezzy, his only real friend back in his normal life. She had distanced herself from him since they returned from the underworld below Newcastle. He missed Ezzy, but he knew she wanted to care for her mother. He hoped she would come back to him one day.

'They took Merek away,' the ghost sitting at Zam's left said. He was a boy ghost no more than eight years old, Zam guessed. Yet he had probably been a ghost for more than a couple of hundred years.

'Was Merek your friend?'

'Yes.'

'Why did they take him away?'

'Because he was different. He wasn't like us anymore.'

'What do you mean?'

The boy turned away from the skeletons and faced Zam for the first time. 'He wasn't dead. They made him dead like us at first. Then they turned him back into a living boy. They couldn't bring us back to life, so they left us here to die again.'

Zam didn't want to think about having to die twice, once as a human and then again as a zombie. 'Who left you?' he asked.

'The Clan.'

'The Clan?'

'Yes, the Cult of the Clan.'

'The Clan?' Bonnyman said.

'Who are the Clan?' Xara asked Bonnyman.

Bonnyman lowered his head. 'They were my employers before I became a zombie.'

'You worked for someone who did things like this to children?'

'I didn't know they did things like this until a moment ago.'

Zam stared at Bonnyman, unsure whether or not to believe him. He turned back towards the child. 'How did they turn you into a... a zombie?' he asked in a gentle voice.

'They made us eat meat,' the ghost boy said. 'They got it from a dead person inside there, before the creature who always cried was kept in the cell.' He pointed at the wall across from them as he spoke. 'I never liked hearing her cry. She always sounded like a child whenever she did.'

Hestia rushed towards the cell and Zam watched her place her hands on the wall, searching for a door or some means of entering.

'Q, come over here and help me find a way of getting into this thing,' Hestia said.

'Go ahead, Q,' Zam said, as he remained sitting with the ghost children.

Q turned around and headed towards Hestia. When he reached her, his lights illuminated the cell wall better, but there was still no visible sign of a doorway. He moved towards the other side of the cell and his light reflected back off something in the wall. Hestia rubbed the wall where the glimmer of light reflected back and, when she finished, a small circular window was revealed. Q raised the light on his armrest and directed it towards the window.

'The glass is so thick I can barely see through it,' Hestia said, peering into the window. 'It must be covered with dirt on the other side too.'

'My scanners can't locate a doorway or any other means of access,' Q said. 'There are two small compartments directly below that window, though.'

Hestia moved her hands across the wall below the window and after a moment Zam heard a clicking noise, then the sound of scraping.

'What is it?' Zam said.

'There were metal panels sealing two compartments,' Hestia said. 'Inside each compartment is a gauntlet made from a flexible kind of metal. I can put my hands inside them.'

Hestia remained silent for a moment.

'What?' Bonnyman asked.

'One of the gloves has a knife, or scalpel attached to it.'

Bonnyman strode over to Hestia and peered into the window. 'We need to get inside.'

'I can have a look inside,' Xara said, walking over to the wall.

'No,' Zam began, but before he could say anything else, Xara had walked through the wall and into the cell.

'I can't see much, it's too dim in here,' they heard Xara say in a muffled voice. 'Hang on, I'll see if I can clean the window. Shine your light in here, Q.'

Xara's hand suddenly appeared through the window.

'Oops,' she said, 'I didn't visualise that very well.'

'Xara hurry up, I don't like you in there alone,' Zam said.

'Is she your girlfriend?' one of the ghost girls asked.

'No… she's just a friend,' Zam said too quickly.

'There, now I can see...' Xara said.

'What is it?' Zam asked.

'There's a body,' Xara said in a low voice, 'but it's not like the children. It's not decomposed. And its hands, they have been cut off.'

Zam watched Hestia and saw her eyes change as she pushed past Q and once more stared into the window.

Without warning, Xara rushed back through the cell wall, bent over and began to wretch like she was going to vomit.

She could not vomit.

Zam crawled over to the cage entrance and pulled himself up by the rails. Then he stumbled across to the operating table, steadied himself and moved over to Xara.

'Xara, what is it?' he said.

'There are two mechanical arms in there. They have butcher-like surgical instruments attached to them. Someone must have been using them to cut up the creature inside the cell. There are bits of its flesh and body parts all over the floor. How could they do that?'

'Don't cry Xara,' Zam said.

'What else am I supposed to do?'

'I don't know. You could... hug me if you want. Just don't cry. I hate hearing you cry.'

Xara raised her head. 'I can't hug anyone anymore.'

Zam thought for a moment. 'You can if you visualise it, like Hestia taught you to open doors.'

Xara hesitated, then slowly raised her arms and held onto Zam.

Zam had never before experienced the sensations he now felt as Xara hugged him. It was like being enveloped in pin prick electricity, like the feeling in your spine when you have experienced something that moves you, only his whole body felt that same way. When they parted, Zam felt like he was going to pass out. He steadied himself and saw that the ghost children had left the cage. They were watching him and Xara.

'How do we leave this place, Zam?' the boy who had talked earlier asked.

'If you could be anywhere you wanted?' Zam said. 'Where would it be?'

'I want to see my mother.'

'Me too,' said the ghost girl who had also spoken.

'We are zombies,' one of the other girls said. 'We belong here and nowhere else.' She turned around and started to walk back towards the cage.

'Wait,' Zam said. 'You are not zombies, you are spirits. And if you are spirits, you can do everything else other spirits can do. There is nothing keeping you here. Nothing but yourselves.'

The girl turned around and faced Zam. 'How do you know that?'

Zam looked at Eufame, understanding another truth for the first time. 'This lady was pregnant when she died. She thinks she belongs here too. She thinks her baby's soul will die if she leaves, but that's not true either.'

Eufame gasped. 'What are you doing?'

'Show her Freya. Show yourself to your mother.'

'I don't know what you mean, Zam.'

'Yes you do, Freya. Now show yourself, show yourself and put an end to the sadness you share with your mother.'

'Zam…' Eufame started.

Zam shook his head and placed his finger against his lips, indicating for Eufame to remain silent.

'Only you can help these children, Freya,' Zam said. 'Not me. Now show them that anything is possible.'

Nothing happened at first, until Eufame jerked forwards, pressing her hands to her stomach. She straightened up, continuing to hold onto her stomach. Then she cried out in pain. 'Zam, what have you done?'

Eufame's screams echoed around the room until her form began to flicker in and out of view. When she stopped flickering, the side of her body stretched out of shape, as if an invisible hand pushed at her from within. Zam was horrified, thinking he had made a mistake. He thought Eufame and Freya were going to pull each other apart. He wanted to shout out loud, to tell Freya to stop what she was doing, but the air seemed to have been sucked out of the room and he could not find his voice. When Eufame closed her eyes tightly shut and her face wrinkled up in agony, Zam moved towards her. The closer he got, the more his lungs started to burn and his head began to spin. Just as he was about to touch Eufame, something flowed out from her ghostly image and began to take shape. A moment later, a young girl stared up at Eufame.

'Mum,' the girl said.

Eufame looked down at Freya as if what she was seeing wasn't real, before she quickly hugged her and started to weep.

The zombie ghost girl stared at Eufame and her daughter. Zam could see that she was thinking deeply and as she continued to think, so her appearance slowly began to change. Her translucent skin no longer looked white and dead. Her cheeks were flushed now and her eyes went from black to blue, while her hair shone, as if the sun touched it on a bright summer's day. She giggled, like only a young girl can giggle and as she stared at Zam, she slowly began to fade, just like the other children were beginning to fade.

'Wait,' Bonnyman yelled. 'How did they make your friend human again?'

The girl looked up to the ceiling and just before she disappeared completely she spoke one last time. 'They made him eat more flesh,' she said. 'Not dead flesh this time. They made him eat the flesh from something that was still alive. He ate flesh from the creature who wept at night.'

Bonnyman stared at the empty space where the ghost children had been moments earlier. Then he turned and stared at Hestia with eyes that looked full of longing.

20

Zam's legs felt like they were about to buckle under his weight. He looked towards Q, ready to ask him to come over so he could sit down, when he saw that Hestia continued to stare through the window into the cell. 'Are you okay?' he asked.

Hestia didn't turn around. 'I know the changeling inside this cell,' she said. 'I need to find a way inside so I can give her a warrior's burial.'

'How do you know?' Xara asked.

'When you picked up her hand I saw a ring on her finger,' Hestia said. 'I recognise the ring.'

Zam left Xara's side, hobbled over to the operating table and leant against it. 'Q, blast a way through that wall,' he said, staring at Hestia, never seeing her look so lost.

'Hestia,' Q said, 'please move aside so I can do some damage to this wall.'

Hestia backed away from the cell and Q used his laser

on the wall, quickly burning a circular hole. When he had finished with the laser, a mechanical fist whirred out of his armrest and it rammed the wall where Q had burned the circle until it crumbled, leaving an entranceway into the cell.

Hestia entered first, followed closely by Bonnyman.

Zam sat down in Q's seat and moved towards the opening in the wall. Shining the light into the cell, Zam saw a cramped space in which Hestia and Bonnyman gathered the body parts of the changeling.

'I think the operating table is detachable,' Zam said. 'We could put your friend on there, Hestia.'

Zam moved aside as Hestia walked over to the operating table and placed her friend's severed hands on it. Bonnyman followed close behind, placing her legs on the table. Zam couldn't help but stare at the body parts. He saw that pieces of flesh had been cut away and guessed the missing flesh had been eaten by Marek. Hestia and Bonnyman entered the cell again and came out a moment later carrying the torso. After placing it on the operating table, Hestia entered the cell one last time alone.

'Why hasn't the body decomposed?' Zam asked Bonnyman. 'It must have been here hundreds of years.'

'It takes thousands of years for changeling flesh to decay,' Bonnyman answered.

Hestia returned a moment later and gently placed her friend's head on the operating table. 'Her name was Gaia,' she said.

Xara lowered her head. 'I'm sorry you had to find her this way.'

'I knew something was wrong, but this...' Hestia said, looking down at what remained of Gaia.

'When did she go missing?' Zam asked.

'Shortly after Isaac killed my uncle and ate him. She went looking for my uncle.'

'He killed your uncle!'

'Yes, my uncle needed killing. He had lost his mind. He was rampaging across Scotland out of control. He was over three thousand years old, who knows what his mind was like.'

'How old are you Hestia?' Xara asked.

'Not quite as old as my uncle when he died.'

Zam stared at Bonnyman. 'Hestia's uncle was the changeling you ate?' he asked.

'Yes,' Bonnyman said, 'his flesh killed me and brought me back to this miserable zombie life.' He watched Hestia closely, like he was seeing more than what she was doing.

'What do you mean?' Zam asked.

'The child spoke of its friend eating live changeling flesh and becoming human again. I ate dead changeling flesh.'

'Is that true, Hestia?' Zam asked.

'Changelings have been hunted throughout time,' she said clasping her hands together as she looked down on Gaia. 'And sometimes eaten too. But this is the first time I have known the flesh of a live changeling to be eaten. If the child said it turned a zombie back into a human, then I believe what the child said to be true.'

Bonnyman continued to stare at Hestia as she talked to Zam.

'I don't understand,' Xara said. 'If this...Cult of the Clan were experimenting with a live changeling, then why did they kill it? Why didn't they turn all of the children back into humans before they did that?'

'That's a very good question,' Bonnyman said, 'changelings are incredibly difficult to capture alive. In fact this is the first changeling I know that has ever been captured alive. I'm not sure how they managed to do that or why they would kill it afterwards.'

Hestia breathed in deeply. 'They cut off Gaia's hand and legs so they could handle her more easily. I don't think they cut off her head. I think she cut off her own head.'

'How could she cut off her own head?' Zam asked.

'For a changeling, it would be easy to cut off one's own head, especially with a surgical saw in the room,' Bonnyman said. 'The real question is: why would it do that?'

'Why would anyone cut off their own head?' Hestia said. 'Other than because the alternative was too horrific to live with?'

Hestia moved to the top of the operating table and motioned Bonnyman to the opposite end of the table. 'It's time we took my mother out of this terrible place,' she said.

It took a moment before Zam realised what Hestia said, when he did, the horror of her words lasted for much longer than a moment.

Hestia lifted the top end of the bed off the frame and waited for Bonnyman to do the same. Once he had, they carried Hestia's mother out of the cell, out of the City of the Dead and back into the underworld.

Hestia buried her mother beneath a copse of underworld cherry trees. As she spoke, blossom from the trees fell like snowflakes on a still day. Zam didn't know if the blossom was a natural phenomenon to the underworld or something invoked by Hestia. It didn't matter; it was perfectly beautiful.

'Mother,' Hestia gently said, before speaking in a musical voice that Zam could not understand in terms of words, but felt vividly as far as feeling could affect.

Freya wept as Hestia spoke and a short while after Hestia said her final words, Freya hugged her mother. 'I think it's time we left,' she said.

Eufame held onto Freya's hand. 'Yes, I think you are right.' She turned to Zam. 'I don't know how to thank you.'

'You don't have to thank me,' Zam said.

Freya rushed over to Zam and hugged him in a ghostly kind of way. 'Thank you anyway,' she said, 'and thank you for saving the children.'

'I think you saved the children, Freya.'

Eufame grabbed her daughter's hand again. 'Come,' she said, 'we have much catching up to do.'

Freya disentangled herself from Zam. 'Are you sure we can't do anything to help Zam?' she asked her mother.

Eufame thought for a moment. 'You could perform a summoning on the doppelganger.'

'A summoning?' Zam said. 'How would I do that?'

'Easy enough; just look into a mirror and call the doppelganger by its name. You do know its name?'

Hestia stood up from her kneeling position by her mother's grave and turned to face Eufame.

'It is too dangerous,' she said. 'Krackle would only show himself if Napoleon was on his own. And this time, he would know to be more careful when dealing with him. I do not know if Napoleon could resist the doppelganger a second time.'

'Doesn't Krackle answer to you?' Zam asked Bonnyman. 'You are his leader, right? Just order him to tell us what he knows.'

Bonnyman stared at Hestia. 'After what the wraith said, I am not sure anyone answers to me anymore.'

'If you can get the doppelganger to stare into a mirror while it's still inside a mirror,' Eufame said, 'then it will be trapped and have to tell you what it knows.'

Bonnyman frowned. 'Krackle is unlikely to fall for an old trick like that.'

'What if Zam entered the mirror by its edge?' Eufame

continued. 'The doppelganger would be unable to touch him and he wouldn't be expecting Zam to have a mirror inside a mirror.'

'That would mean Napoleon entering the mirror, which holds other, far worse dangers,' Hestia said.

'What's the difference between a mirror and a mirrors edge?' Zam asked.

Eufame looked uneasily from Hestia to Zam. 'Entering a mirror by its edge would place you in a different plain of existence to anyone who entered a mirror by its face. You would be like a ghost inside the mirror.'

'I vote we go in by the mirror's edge,' Q said.

'Couldn't Krackle just step out of the mirror's face and then enter by its edge the same as Zam?' Xara asked.

'A doppelganger can only leave a mirror by absorbing someone who is staring into the mirror.'

'What does a doppelganger do once it has absorbed someone?' Zam asked.

Hestia answered the question before Eufame could speak. 'It becomes the person it absorbs, until it gets bored, then it returns to a mirror, until it gets bored again. Then it looks for someone it views as worthy to take over their life. It's a never ending circle with doppelgangers.'

'Does the person it absorbed come back once it returns to the mirror?' Xara asked.

'Once someone is absorbed by a doppelganger, they no longer exist.'

'If Zam is a ghost inside a mirror, then the doppelganger

187

won't be able to absorb him when he enters the mirrors edge, right?' Xara asked.

Hestia sighed. 'Stepping inside a mirror is like stepping into Pandora's Box. It is a world of illusion and fragility. If the mirror is broken then so, too, will be whoever is inside the mirror at the time it is broken.'

'Then we will have to ensure nothing happens to the mirror once Zam enters it,' Bonnyman said. 'I for one want to know who is behind this and Krackle appears to be our only way of discovering who that might be.'

Hestia was about to say something when Zam spoke. 'How do I enter a mirror edge anyway?' he said.

'There is only one way to do that – you need a spirit to open a doorway,' Eufame said.

'And once I'm inside, how do I get back out?'

'You need a spirit to open a doorway again.'

'How will this spirit know when it's time to open the doorway?'

'The spirit needs to be inside the mirror with you.'

'Will you come into the mirror with me, Eufame?' Zam asked.

Eufame looked sad. 'I'm sorry, I can't. I'm afraid that if I did, I would be taken away from you before you had finished doing what you need to do.'

'What do you mean?'

'You have freed Eufame from the hold this world had upon her,' Hestia said. 'The light calls to both her and Freya. It could take them at any time.'

'I'll go with you, Zam,' Xara said.

Zam frowned. 'It's too dangerous for you to come with me.'

'Then it's too dangerous for you, too.'

'Do you even know how to open a mirror edge doorway?'

'No, but I'm sure Eufame can show me.'

'A spirit needs only to touch a mirror edge and a doorway will open,' Eufame said.

'See, it's easy,' Xara said. 'All we need now is a mirror.'

'Two mirrors,' Eufame corrected her.

Hestia walked up to Zam and rested her hand on his shoulder. 'I don't like this plan.'

'Sometimes we don't have a choice,' Zam said. 'You've told me that often enough yourself.'

Hestia gently squeezed Zam's shoulder. 'I could choose to stop you.'

'Can you guarantee I won't be killed when I'm next attacked?' Zam said. 'Because there is going to be a next time, unless we discover who is behind all of this.'

'I promised your grandfather I would keep you from harm.'

'I don't think you should have made that promise, not in these circumstances. The best way for you to keep your promise, is to let me try and find out what we are dealing with before the next attack.'

Hestia sighed. 'Do not stay longer than you have to inside mirror's edge. Glass is like a heart. It has a fragile nature. It is easily broken.'

'I promise I'll be in and out as quickly as I can. And that's a promise I intend to keep.'

'And I promise to do my best to see no one breaks the mirror once you have entered.'

'Who would want to break the mirror?'

'Apart from the assassins who want to see you dead, there are others who would do it just for the hell of it.' She turned towards Bonnyman. 'And there are others who I simply do not trust any longer.'

Hestia had been subdued since finding her mother's body in the City of the Dead. Zam didn't want to disturb her but he had too many unanswered questions buzzing inside his head, eventually he needed them answering. 'Tell me about the Cult of the Clan,' Zam said to her.

'The Cult is something you do not want to become involved with,' Hestia replied.

They were waiting by the trees opposite Bonnyman's tent, while he arranged for the mirrors to be brought to them. The night gaunts skulked around the tent and they too seemed to be waiting for something to happen. Zam eyed them warily; he had never seen anything look so hungry all the time. He had a feeling they were driven by nothing more than their appetite. 'It looks like I am already involved with them,' he said.

Hestia drank from the water canister before replying. 'The Cult is an ancient sect that has been around for as long as man has been around.'

'I've never heard of them.'

'That is how they like to keep things. They are more secretive than the creatures of the underworld.'

'They are more secret than I ever imagined,' Bonnyman said, as he approached from behind Zam.

Zam jumped, surprised Bonnyman could sneak up on him like that. 'Why did you work for them?' he asked, trying not to let Bonnyman see how he had startled him.

'They paid me well,' Bonnyman replied, 'and the work they wanted me to do was always interesting. I did not know they had figured out how to catch a live changeling, though.'

'The changeling you are talking about was my mother,' Hestia said, obviously annoyed with Bonnyman.

'They killed more than they caught alive,' Bonnyman said.

'How many changelings are left, Hestia?' Zam asked.

'On these isles, there is only one who remains alive.'

Zam was shocked by Hestia's answer. 'What about elsewhere?'

'There are perhaps a dozen or so worldwide that I know about. I do not know if all of them are still alive after what I have just learned about the Cult.'

Bonnyman looked like he was thinking about something important. He turned towards Hestia. 'If what the zombie child said is true, then you are the only remaining changeling on these isles who can make me human again.'

'So it seems,' Hestia said.

'You'd have to eat Hestia alive if you want to become human again,' Zam said, 'and you are never going to do that.'

Bonnyman looked past Zam. 'Your mirror is here,' he said.

Zam turned around and saw one of the night gaunts standing on its hind legs carrying a large mirror and heading towards them.

'It is time to prepare for your encounter with Krackle,' Bonnyman said. 'Time to see what you are made of.'

Zam didn't like the way Bonnyman looked at him when he spoke. When the night gaunt stopped in front of Bonnyman, the zombie instructed it to place a cover over the mirror that he got from the tent earlier. He then walked over to the edge of the trees and Zam felt a shift in the underworld as a flat ridge appeared beneath Bonnyman's feet and the moorland in front of him morphed into a vast plane of empty desert.

'The way he does that is so damn cool,' Zam said as he watched Bonnyman transform the underworld landscape. 'Can you do the same in the Angle underworld, Hestia?'

'Yes, all underworld leaders have the ability to terra-form their realm.'

'It's the perfect landscape,' Bonnyman said when he finished. 'Krackle will see there is no one for miles around when he gazes out of the mirror. All he will see is the boy.'

'What if there is a high wind and it blows the mirror off the ridge?' Zam said.

'There will be no wind today,' Bonnyman replied.

Zam held onto the mirror and attempted to rock it from side to side. It seemed stable enough. 'Are you sure Krackle will come once I am on my own?' he asked Hestia.

'Apart from his original reason for wanting you dead,' Hestia said, 'you hurt his pride when you escaped him. I am sure he will want to regain some semblance of revenge.'

Eufame's ghostly hand touched Zam's shoulder. 'I wish I could go inside the mirror with you,' she said.

'It's okay,' Zam said. 'I understand why you can't.'

'How does this work, Eufame?' Xara asked, 'I just touch the edge of the mirror and a doorway appears?'

'There is a little more to it than that, you have to visualise the doorway inside your head, like most things you want to interact with in the physical plane, now that you are a ghost.'

'Will this doppelganger know if I try to open the doorway now? I'd like to practice before I have to do it when it matters.'

'As long as the face of the mirror is covered, it will be fine,' Hestia said.

Xara put her hand beneath the sheet covering the edge of the mirror and hesitantly touched the mirror's edge. As soon as she did, a portal appeared at the edge of the mirror. It swirled like clouds being sucked into a tornado, yet everything around it remained perfectly still.

'This isn't quite what I visualised,' she said.

'Are you certain we can enter through that?' Zam asked. 'It looks kinda wild.'

'Yes you can enter there,' Eufame said, 'but you need to do so quickly, so the doppelganger does not disappear before you see it inside the mirror. Once you see him, he will be held inside the mirror, unable to leave until you leave.'

'How is Xara going to open the portal without Krackle realising what's going on?'

'Use your initiative,' Bonnyman said.

Zam snorted. 'Thanks, that really helps.'

'Try to distract the doppelganger first,' Hestia said.

'How do I do that?' Zam asked.

'Use your initiative,' Q said. 'I find that when I do, things just drop into place.'

'When have you ever used your initiative?' Zam asked.

'Just now, when I told you to use yours.'

'I think it's time you all left,' Zam said. 'I have something important to do and I'm sure you all do, too.'

'Whatever happens,' Hestia said, 'do not let Krackle touch you before you enter the mirror. The risk is too great. Do not be afraid to fail, back away from him if you have to. We will find another way of learning who is behind all of this.'

'Don't worry, Hestia. I know what a doppelganger is capable of doing to me. The thing is, Krackle doesn't know what I am capable of doing to him.'

Bonnyman walked over to Zam and handed him a silver disc covered in an ornate basket weave design. 'Keep this hidden until the time is right to use it.'

Zam took the disc from him, turning it in his hands until he saw a small silver fastener. He pressed it and the cover sprung open, revealing the circular mirror inside. 'Thank you,' he said.

'Once the doppelganger is inside a mirror reflection – inside a mirror,' Eufame said, 'he will be unable to absorb anyone. All of his powers will be mute.'

'He will still be able to talk, though?' Zam said.

'Yes, and I'm sure he will be angry, too.'

'Enough,' Bonnyman said, 'let's get this over with.' Without waiting for anyone to reply, he walked off with the night gaunt on all fours following close at his heels. The others said their goodbyes to Zam and left in the same direction as Bonnyman. Watching his companions leave, Zam waited until they were out of sight and then turned towards the mirror.

'Are you sure you are ready for this?' Xara asked.

'Zam is ready,' Q said. 'He's a Lion of the Wood. They are always ready.'

'A Lion of the Wood?' Xara said.

Zam shrugged his shoulders. 'It's a long story.'

'You must tell me about it when this is over.'

'Yes,' Zam said, 'but first, you need to make yourself scarce so that Krackle can't see...'

'Done,' Xara said, before Zam could say anymore.

Zam couldn't see Xara. He looked behind the mirror. He still couldn't see her. 'When did you learn how to turn invisible?' he asked.

'Eufame has been teaching me a few tricks,' Xara said.

Zam stared at the side of the mirror in the direction where Xara's voice came from. 'How can you be invisible from me? I could see Eufame when she was invisible and everyone else couldn't see her.'

'I'm not sure.'

Zam thought for a moment before speaking. 'You are different to the other ghosts I have known.'

'What do you mean?'

'For one, you can hide from me. For another, when you whisper in my ear and when we hug. I don't know... Maybe it would be the same if other ghosts did that to me too.'

'I'm not different, Zam. I am always going to look the same. Eufame said her appearance has never changed since the day she died. I don't like knowing I will remain this way forever.'

'You won't, I'm sure. When you cross over I mean. I'm sure a soul can be anything it wants to be, any shape or size, once it crosses over. A bit like a changeling, only cooler.' Zam didn't like to think about losing Xara. He wondered why he felt so attached to her so quickly.

197

'What if I never cross over? What if I remain a ghost forever?'

'You will cross over when the time is right.'

'How can you be so sure?'

'Because you are... someone I really like. I can't imagine anything happening to you other than you being with your parents.'

'I still can't understand why I didn't cross over when I first died, like my parents did.'

'If I was to guess, I think you are still here because of the circumstances of your death and because your soul is not ready to pass over. I think you must have something it wants to do before it crosses over.'

'Maybe Xara's soul is like me and wants to see what it's like to be a ghost for a little while,' Q said. 'Or more likely, it has something to do with you Zam. I've seen the way Xara stares at you at night when you are sleeping.'

'How does she stare at me?' Zam asked.

'Like I would if I ever found that bomb disposal unit I told you about?'

'A bomb disposal unit?' Xara said.

'His dream girl is a bomb disposal unit,' Zam said.

'Oh.'

'Isn't it time you removed the cover from the mirror?' Q said.

Zam positioned himself in front of the mirror. 'Yes I think it is. First, though, we need a signal, so that Xara knows when to open the mirror's edge.'

'How about on your marks, get set, go?' Q said.

Zam looked down at Q. 'I'm not sure that will work. I have a feeling Krackle will know we are up to something.'

'Why don't you sneeze?' Xara said.

Zam shook his head from side to side. 'When you see me touch the mirror, that's the signal for you to open the mirror edge, Xara.'

'Won't that be dangerous?' Xara said. 'Won't that give the doppelganger the opportunity to pull you into the mirror?'

'Yes, but it will also distract him. He won't be expecting me to touch the mirror.'

'Oh,' Q said.

'Okay, no more discussion, it's time we did this. Xara, are you standing by the mirror's edge?'

'Yes, I'm ready, Zam.'

'Q, keep quiet, I don't want you scaring Krackle away.'

'Why would he be scared of me?'

'He probably hasn't come across a talking wheelchair before. I don't expect there are many in the underworld.'

'Good point.'

'Okay, here we go,' Zam said, pulling the cover away from the mirror.

As soon as he removed the sheet, the top half of Krackle's body loomed out of the mirror, grabbing hold of Zam by the shoulders and pulling him towards the mirror.

'Q, reverse!' Zam yelled.

Q responded immediately and his wheels began to turn backwards, but made no impression as they spun in the dirt, unable to get any grip.

'You were lucky last time,' Krackle said, 'this time you won't be so lucky.'

Zam stared at the featureless doppelganger and for a brief moment he thought everything was lost as its grip on his arms felt firm and unyielding. Zam tried to wrench himself from the doppelganger and Xara appeared at his side, grabbing hold of him, pulling against the doppelganger's force.

'Get your hands off him,' she yelled.

Krackle turned to face Xara and hissed at her.

Xara hissed back at the doppelganger and Zam wanted to do nothing more than laugh out loud at the ridiculousness of the situation. He didn't, though, because Krackle had renewed his efforts to pull Zam into the mirror and the doppelganger's grip on his arms tightened until it felt like they were going to be squeezed off him. With Q and Xara pulling him in the opposite direction, it also felt like he was going to be torn in half and Zam screamed out in pain and frustration. Hearing the familiar whirring come from Q's armrest, he turned around to see one of Q's mechanical arms fly past his head.

'Gaze into this, doppelganger,' Q said, pressing a small mirror into Krackle's face.

When the mirror touched him, it was Krackle's turn to yell out in pain as he pulled away from the mirror and Zam saw that it had burned the doppelganger where it touched his face. However, Krackle continued to hold onto Zam just as tightly as he had before. Zam wished he had Grandfather's steam shaver with him or that he hadn't been so close to the mirror when he removed the cover. He tried desperately to pull himself from Krackle's grip, but the doppelganger was incredibly strong and Zam started to slowly move towards the mirror once more. When Q tried to burn Krackle with the mirror again, the doppelganger released one of his hands from Zam and grabbed hold of Q's mechanical arm, twisting it away from him. With one of his arms now free, Zam punched the doppelganger in the face but instead of gaining any advantage, he yelled out in pain as soon as he connected with Krackle.

It was like punching the hardest diamond.

Another one of Q's motors whirred into life and a mechanical arm with a circular saw attached to the end of it popped out of his other arm rest, heading for the doppelganger. Krackle responded by pushing Zam's arm towards the saw and Q pulled back just before the saw sliced into Zam's arm. Wasting no time, Krackle immediately pressed his face into Zam's and started to absorb him. With a look of horror on her face, Xara turned towards the mirror and touched its edge with one hand while continuing to hold onto Zam with the other.

As soon as her hand touched the mirror, the doppelganger turned around. When he saw the portal, his eyes – that now looked like Zam's eyes, widened and he released his grip on Zam, pulling himself back into the mirror. At the same time, Xara stepped into the portal and she was instantly sucked into the mirror's edge, along with Zam, who she still held onto, and Q.

It took a moment for Zam to realise what had happened. At first he thought Krackle had pulled him into the mirror rather than Xara. Staring at the doppelganger staring back at him, he knew that wasn't the case. Krackle stood featureless and bland, yet Zam could see by his body language that he was far from pleased. Being inside the mirror's edge suddenly hit him, as the cold, still air painfully entered his lungs. It felt like he was breathing ice, rather than air. After a moment, there was no pain and the air tasted like glass coated in sweetened lemon. Looking down at his chest he saw that his whole body was translucent, just like Xara's, who stood at his side.

'You're a ghost like me now, Zam,' she said. 'How does it feel?'

Her hand no longer felt electrical, it no longer felt like a ghost hand. Inside mirror's edge, it felt like smoothest glass.

'It feels weird,' Zam said, standing up. He lifted one leg, then the other. 'My legs are normal.' He turned to his left and saw Bonnyman's underworld at the other side of the mirror. It was like looking through a window, only what he saw on the other side looked intensely colourful, more so than how he remembered it being when he was actually standing there a moment ago. Inside the mirror, the underworld looked like a colour saturated dreamscape.

'I look like a ghost,' Q said. 'I actually look like a ghost. Is this what it feels like to be a ghost, Xara?'

'Not exactly,' Xara said.

Zam stared at the doppelganger. 'You can't move, can you?' Zam said. 'You are trapped while we are here.'

'And you can't stay here forever,' Krackle replied. 'Soon you will have to leave. There is nothing inside a mirror for the likes of you.'

'Why do you want to become me?' Zam said.

'I don't want to become you.'

'You tried to absorb me.'

'And afterwards I would have discarded your form, like I would an unwanted child.'

'You aren't the only one trying to kill me.'

'You are obviously not a popular human.'

'And you are not popular with Isaac Bonnyman. He doesn't like it when his underlings do things without his permission.'

Krackle shook his head from side to side. 'Bonnyman is a fool. He is no leader of mine. He cannot even see that his kingdom is no longer his kingdom.'

'Whose kingdom is it then, yours?'

Krackle crouched down and picked up a stone that looked more like a diamond and passed it from one hand to the next. 'There are too few of us in my world to call it a kingdom anymore.'

'You're not the only one who thinks the underworld is coming to an end.'

'God has forsaken us. He has abandoned us like He abandons everything.'

'Everything must come to an end.'

Krackle stood up. 'Not like this. Not without a fight.'

'Fight who?'

'Not who, what.'

'What then?'

'Death of course. In the end, the final battle is always with death.'

'You want to live forever?'

'I want a choice. I don't want to become no more because some God who doesn't listen or speak decides it is time for my kind to cease to exist.'

Zam had a thought. 'You are working for the Cult of the Clan, aren't you?'

'I never said that…' Krackle said, too quickly.

'It doesn't matter if you did. When I spread the word that you are giving away their secrets, I'm sure you can guess what will happen to you. We know they are experimenting with changelings. Maybe you know about that too?'

'I know nothing about anything.'

'And I know you are not working on your own. It's too much of a coincidence that I have been attacked by you and a wraith within days of each other.'

'Do what you must human.'

'There is only one thing left for me to do,' Zam said, taking the mirror from his pocket, 'I am going to show this to the Clan.' He pressed the fastener on the mirror and the cover immediately sprang open. Once the mirror opened up inside the mirror edge, it began to sing like a melancholic choir of cellos.

'What have you done?' Krackle yelled, as he stared at the mirror. Unable to turn away from it, he clamped his hands over ears that Zam could not see. It looked like he was screaming, yet no sound came from his mouth as the mirror continued to sing. Krackle's silent shrieks remained uninterrupted as his form slowly began to stretch and elongate as he was drawn towards the mirror. When he first touched it, the mirror trembled in Zam's hand while Krackle was sucked into the mirror like water spiralling down a plug hole until nothing remained of the doppelganger but a screaming form inside the small mirror Zam held in his hands.

'I've beaten you again, Krackle. That's what I've done,' Zam said as he clamped the mirror shut with the doppelganger trapped inside.

As soon as he shut the mirror, the music coming from it stopped.

'That was beautiful,' Q said. 'The mirror was... Open

it again, Zam, I need to hear it one more time.'

Zam was surprised at how desperate Q sounded.

'It was like the mirror was singing to me alone, no one else in the entire world but me,' Xara said.

'Open the mirror so we can hear it sing again,' Q repeated.

'I can't,' Zam said. 'I think the mirror is casting some type of charm over you. I think we'd all be trapped like Krackle is trapped if we listened to it again.'

'Is that such a bad thing?' Q said.

'Yes it is,' Zam said. 'I almost didn't close it. It was charming me too.'

'What made you close it?' Xara asked.

'The look on Krackle's face when I saw him trapped inside the mirror.'

'How did he look?'

Zam hesitated, but the words came from his mouth as if he had no choice but to say them. 'He looked like you, Xara, when the wraith flicked the switched and your parents died.'

Zam wished he hadn't reminded Xara about her parents. He could see she was upset again. 'That was quick thinking, Xara,' he said, 'opening the portal and freeing me from Krackle. Thank you.'

He wasn't sure Xara heard him speak.

She touched the mirror edge without responding and the portal opened once more. As they entered it together, they were sucked through and found themselves back in Bonnyman's underworld a moment later. Zam remembered the changes in the air when he went through the ghost door leading from the underworld into the City of the Dead below Edinburgh, how the air in his own world seemed dirty compared to the underworld. Now the air in the underworld seemed dry and stale, not crisp and clean like it was in the mirror. It seemed like every time he went into a different world, so the previous one appeared bland in comparison. He wanted to hear the mirror sing again. He wanted it so much he almost asked

Xara to open the portal so that he could step back into the mirror's edge and open up the small mirror once more.

The noise he heard coming from behind the mirror made him look in that direction, instead and he was shocked to see a wyrm, as black as a night spent in pain, desperately fighting off a mass of night gaunts that surrounded it. The gaunts attached themselves to the wyrm's legs with their bared teeth, stopping it from getting airborne. Flying above the wyrm were a dozen or so bony creatures – human in form, with wide, fragile looking wings and a single curved horn at the side of their heads. The creatures crashed into the wyrm and knocked it back onto the ground whenever it managed to free itself from the gaunts and become airborne. White fire spurted from the wyrm's mouth and one of the flying creatures above it burst into flame and then dropped to the ground like an angel falling from grace. Each time the wyrm incinerated one of the creatures, so another replaced it, spawning from the space left by the burning creature. *'The underworld looks after its leader,'* Zam remembered Hestia saying, as he watched the wyrm slowly being forced backwards towards the mirror. He suddenly noticed Bonnyman, standing behind the night gaunts, driving them on towards the wyrm. Just as Zam wondered why the zombie was fighting a wyrm, he caught sight of Eufame sweeping her scythe into the night gaunts, while the butcher ghost sliced them with the meat cleaver. Freya stood behind her mother, holding on to her dress, looking absolutely terrified.

It was then that Zam realised what was happening. 'Q, take me to Hestia, we need to help her,' he said.

'Where is she?' Q asked.

'She's the wyrm Bonnyman is attacking,' Zam said.

Q responded by morphing into the spearhead shaped craft he had transformed into when they flew to the Wicca coven and Zam immediately guided them towards the battle. As they neared Hestia, he saw hundreds of dead night gaunts and the flying creatures scattered across the ground around her. Despite the amount she had killed and continued to kill, they never seemed to decrease in number as more night gaunts rose from the earth beneath just as fast as they were slayed.

'Do not kill her!' Bonnyman yelled. 'I need her weakened, not dead.'

'What are you doing, you crazy zombie?' Zam yelled at Bonnyman as he flew overhead.

Bonnyman glanced towards Zam. 'Keep out of this,' he yelled back, 'this is between me and the changeling.'

Zam was amazed at the clinical way Hestia fought off her attackers, but he could see she was beginning to lose her strength. Eufame and the butcher ghost too, looked overwhelmed by the mass of night gaunt teeth snapping at them.

'We need to clear the area of those damn gaunts,' Zam said to Q.

'We need a nuclear warhead,' Q replied.

'Are you armed with one?'

'No, but your grandfather did equip me with an adjustable head rest.'

'What does Bonnyman think he's doing?' Xara asked.

Zam turned around and saw Xara floating next to him. 'You can fly...'

'I'm not sure if this is flying. I just visualised myself next to you and here I am.'

'It looks like Bonnyman is extremely hungry,' Q said. 'I think he wants to eat Hestia alive.'

'Q, it's time for a light display. Arm your lasers,' Zam said.

'What can I do to help?' Xara asked.

'Whatever you can,' Zam said, as he guided Q towards the gaunts, cutting a path through them with the lasers. The gaunts were sliced into pieces as the lasers swept through their ranks and, for a brief moment, it looked like the battle could be won. When another wave of gaunts rose from beneath the blood soaked bodies of their fallen kin, Zam knew the battle was far from over.

'This is hopeless,' Zam said, seeing yet more of the gaunts rise and immediately begin to attack Hestia. 'We need to do something about Bonnyman.'

Guiding Q directly at Bonnyman, Zam attempted to knock him to the ground, but the zombie stooped just as Zam was about to hit him. Zam swung around planning to do the same again and saw that two of the flying creatures had broken away from the attack on Hestia and were heading directly for him. Hestia saw what was happening and she unleashed a stream of white flame towards the creatures. They dropped from the sky still burning when they hit the earth below. Two more creatures immediately appeared in their place and headed towards Zam. He fired the lasers at them, but missed as the creatures swerved in opposite directions, flanking Zam. Spinning Q onto his side, Zam flew between the creatures, then guided Q downwards, heading directly for Bonnyman. He aimed the lasers at the zombie's head. The laser missed, but its arc sliced through the zombie's wrist, cutting off his hand. The hand dropped to the floor, still gripping the axe it held onto and the zombie leader of the Picts calmly put the bloodied stump into his trench coat pocket as he continued to direct the gaunts in their attack on Hestia.

Distracted for a moment, Zam forgot about the two creatures chasing him and by the time he saw one of them flying at him, it was too late to move out of the way. The creature crashed into the side of Q with a sickening jar, spinning Q out of control. Zam desperately pulled back on Q's controls, attempting to direct them upwards, but before he could regain control, they crashed to the ground and came to a juddering stop behind Bonnyman. The zombie strode over to them and pulled Zam from Q with his remaining hand and then dragged him across the floor to face Hestia.

'I have the boy,' he yelled. 'It's over, Hestia.'

Zam grabbed hold of Bonnyman's arm, attempting to release himself from the zombie's grip but Bonnyman bent into Zam and head-butted him. Dazed, Zam stopped struggling and Bonnyman threw him onto the ground.

'Stay still child or I will have my pets eat you while you cower in the mud.'

Zam stared straight ahead and as his vision began to return to normal, he saw the axe on the floor. Bonnyman's severed hand still gripped the axe. Around him, the noise of battle ceased. He heered Q's motors whirring. Turning around, he saw his friend bent and mangled in the underworld dirt attempting to shift into a recognisable shape. It looked like Q was too damaged to repair himself. Zam began to work through his options when Xara appeared at his side.

'Zam, are you alright?' she said.

He didn't want to use her as an option. He didn't want her to kill again. She had been through too much already. He thought about the butcher ghost. He would always be bad, Freya had told him that. Inside his mind, Zam visualised being inside the butcher ghosts mind and he called upon the ghost to come to his side.

'Shift into the shape of a kriung,' Bonnyman said to Hestia. 'I don't want to eat you in your current shape.'

Hestia sighed heavily and in her current wyrm form it sounded like a furnace had been fed more firewood. 'Let Napoleon leave first.'

'The boy is no threat to me. He is free to leave whenever he wants.'

The butcher ghost appeared next to Zam as Hestia stared to morph into a kriung. It stared down at him and Zam sat up staring back.

'Kill the zombie,' Zam whispered.

He didn't know if the butcher ghost's axe would be able to cut into Bonnyman. He knew something that would, though. 'Take the axe and chop the zombie's head off,' he said, pointing at Bonnyman's axe on the floor.

The butcher ghost looked down at the axe and, at first, Zam thought it didn't know what he wanted it to do. However, when it bent down and attempted to pick up the axe, he knew it understood perfectly. Seeing the ghost's hand pass through the axe, Zam was unconcerned. He knew what to say to the ghost next.

'You have to visualise picking up the axe in your mind. Visualise it like you visualise that shroud you use to cover all the bad things you have done in the past.'

Zam was grateful of the shroud when he looked inside the butcher ghost's thoughts. He didn't want to see the badness the ghost kept hidden from himself and others.

The butcher ghost stared at Zam like it was about to hack off his head. Turning back towards the axe, it picked it up, pulling Bonnyman's hand from it and dropping the hand on the floor. Then it turned towards Bonnyman, walked over to the zombie and started to hack at his neck with the axe.

Zam was dismayed to see that Bonnyman could touch the butcher ghost as if he wasn't a ghost. He grabbed the ghost with his one remaining hand, stopping it from chopping him with the axe and started to eat the ghost's arm. The butcher ghost tried to chop Bonnyman's side with the meat cleaver which it held in its other hand, but a night gaunt jumped up at him and grabbed hold of his hand between its brutal maws.

'I have to help,' Xara said.

'No!' Zam yelled.

Xara ignored Zam and ran towards Bonnyman. Jumping on his back, she grabbed hold of his hair and pulled his head away from the butcher ghost. Bonnyman attempted to shake Xara off his back, but she held onto him with her legs clamped around his waist and her arms around his neck, as she continued to pull his head back like she was trying to pull it off. With Bonnyman fighting off Xara, the butcher ghost managed to free himself and instead of trying to chop off Bonnyman's head, he dropped the meat cleaver, grabbed hold of the zombie's remaining hand and chopped it off with the axe. He then turned his attention to the night gaunt, which still had its jaws clamped around his arm. The butcher ghost raised the axe and cut into the gaunt until it stopped moving and slumped to the floor.

Zam was surprised to see the other night gaunts strangely cowed as they watched their leader fighting ghosts. Bonnyman yelled out in rage, spinning around and around as he tried to throw Xara from his back. The butcher ghost knelt into Bonnyman as he spun around and chopped at his legs with the axe as Xara continued to hang onto the zombie, until his legs gave way and he sank to his knees with his handless arms hanging limp at his side. Xara dropped off Bonnyman's back and before he could respond, she grabbed his arms and held them behind his back.

'Do it now,' she yelled at the butcher ghost. 'Hurry!'

The butcher ghost moved into Bonnyman, hacking at the zombie's neck with the axe. Bonnyman tried to pull away, but Xara leant back into the ground, continuing to hold onto his arms and pressing her feet into Bonnyman's back so that he found it impossible to move. The butcher ghost grabbed hold of Bonnyman's hair and started to hack at his neck once more.

Zam stared at Bonnyman, surprised that he no longer fought back, like he had accepted his fate.

'My dreams have been haunted by this death,' Bonnyman whispered to Zam, just before the butcher ghost swung the axe one more time and the Lord of the Picts head was no longer part of his body.

The butcher ghost stood there for a moment holding onto Bonnyman's head by his hair. Zam looked at Bonnyman's eyes and knew it still wasn't over. 'Feed it to the gaunts,' he said to the butcher ghost.

Bonnyman remained silent as the butcher ghost threw his head towards the gaunts. Zam watched the head slowly spin in the air until it hit the ground and rolled a few feet before coming to a rest with Bonnyman's eyes facing towards the sky. The gaunts did not move until Bonnyman blinked and then they charged at his head and ripped it apart, eating every scrap of his skull and brain. As they ate, the gaunts began to fade along with the on looking creatures that circled above, until finally, neither night gaunt, the flying creatures or Bonnyman's head remained.

Leaves started to fall in the Pict underworld. They didn't fall from trees, they fell from the sky. Red, autumn leaves along with green, spring leaves and black leaves that Zam didn't recognise. When they first appeared, hundreds and thousands fell like snowflakes in the night and left the ground covered in a moving sheet of colour as they rippled in the gentle breeze.

'It's beautiful,' Xara said as she gazed at the leaves falling all around her.

Zam knew the leaves had something to do with him. He didn't know what until Hestia spoke. She had morphed back into the form of the young girl with long, black hair. She walked over to Zam and held onto his hand as she watched the leaves continue to fall.

'It is a passing over,' Hestia said.

'What do you mean?'

'You are the new Lord of this underworld realm. You are the leader of the Picts.'

'Me? That's crazy, why me?'

'You killed the last Lord. You killed Isaac.'

'I didn't kill him, the butcher ghost and... Xara.' He didn't want to think about Xara's part in Bonnyman's death.

'You commanded them to kill Isaac.'

'Wait, this is wrong. I can't be the Lord of any underworld realm.'

'The underworld has chosen you.'

'How do you know it's chosen me?'

'Do you not recognise the leaves?'

'No, not at all,' Zam said. But as soon as the words left his mouth, he started to understand. He started to remember.

***

He was five years old. He could walk then, not as well as all the other children, but better than he could a year or so later when he was first introduced to a wheelchair. It was autumn and the leaves were falling as they walked through the park.

'Xyz, Xyz, Xyz,' Zam said inside his head, not wanting to see any more memories from that day.

It didn't work – the memories wanted him to see.

He remembered holding onto his mother's hand. She was telling him about the meaning of autumn, how it was a transition from summer to winter. How things never end, but instead turned in circles.

Three men stood side-by-side blocking the path up ahead. Zam's mother stopped walking when she saw them.

'Leave the child and come with us,' one of the men said.

'We won't harm him if you do,' another added.

'We will have no choice but to harm him in a grotesque manner if you do not leave the child and come with us,' the third man finished.

Zam stared at the men knowing there was something wrong with them. They looked like men in a vague kind of way, but as he continued to stare, he realised they were not men. They were monsters dressed like men, with stretched, wire like skin and manic eyes.

His mother bent down, holding his head in her hand, turning him away from the monsters that were dressed like men. She kissed him on the forehead. 'Remember, Zam,' she said, – his mother had been the first one to call him Zam – 'there are no endings, just circles. You must be brave. You must go home alone. Go by the bandstand and across the bridge so that you don't have to cross the road.'

She stood up then and walked towards the men.

Zam ran after her.

His mother stopped walking and held onto him. He had his eyes closed. He thought no one could take her away from him if he couldn't see them do it. A moment later he felt gentle, light hands pulling at him and his mother slipped away from his grasp. He opened his eyes. One of the monsters was bleeding. It bled black blood. Its blood covered the leaves where it stood, turning them black. His mother held a weapon, like a knife, but not a knife. It was more like a ribcage bone that had been shaped into a knife. Zam was thrown to the floor by the monster that was bleeding. It took the weapon off his mother and the four of them walked away from Zam.

'Mum,' Zam shouted.

His mother never looked back as she began to fade and then eventually disappeared like a blurred memory, along with the three monsters that flanked her.

Zam opened his eyes and stared at Hestia. 'How could I forget?' he asked.

'I'm sorry,' Hestia said. 'You were hysterical when you came home. We used underworld magic to calm you. Maybe it clouded your memories of that day. Maybe it was the trauma of what you saw. I can't say for sure.'

'"We"? Who are "we"?'

'Your father, your grandfather and me.'

Too many questions raced through Zam's mind. 'I have only seen my father perhaps a dozen times since that day.'

'He searches for your mother.'

'Tell me what happened to my mother,' he said. 'Tell me the truth this time.'

'We never knew who took her away. Even now, I'm not sure.'

'Even now?'

'I never thought so at the time, but now I'm beginning to wonder if the Clan were involved.'

'The Clan. Why would they be interested in my mother?'

'Your mother is half-changeling.'

'How is that possible?'

'Your mother is my daughter.'

'You and Grandfather...' Zam said.

'Yes,' Hestia said. 'We are husband and wife.'

'I don't understand.'

'We needed to protect you. Your grandfather wanted to keep the underworld out of your life. When your mother was taken, we agreed that I should leave him and return to my father in the underworld below Newcastle. There would be no reason for anyone to come after you then.'

'What about my father? Is he a changeling too?'

'No.'

'What is he then?'

'He is a man.'

Zam's head began to pound as if it was about to explode. 'What about all the presents and the emails that my mother sends me?'

'I'm sorry. That was your grandfather. Please don't be angry with him, he thought he was doing the right thing. He only ever wanted you to be happy. He has always wanted that.'

'You are my grandmother,' Zam still couldn't believe it. 'You were going to kill me in the underworld below Newcastle.'

'No, I could never do that.'

'But Rat, you killed Rat.'

'In battle, sometimes we do things in the heat of the moment.'

Zam heard Q moving behind him. He turned around. Q almost looked like a wheelchair. A mangled wheelchair.

'This is the best I can do,' Q said. 'We need to get back to your grandfather's workshop for some repairs.'

Zam climbed into Q's seat and buckled himself in, noticing Eufame and Freya standing beside Xara and the butcher ghost. They were all staring at him. As he stared back at them, underworld creatures began to appear all around them: werebeasts, elf-like beings, half-human, half-beast creatures, spirits, wraiths, skeletal figures that flickered in and out of vision as he stared at them... In the sky above, wyrms flew with dark shadows and feathered, stick-like creatures he could not name.

'What's happening?' Zam asked Hestia.

'The Pict underworld is paying tribute to its new lord,' Hestia said.

'I'm not their lord.'

'It doesn't look like anyone is prepared to challenge you.'

'Challenge me?'

'Yes, if another thinks you are unworthy they can

challenge your authority. They can only do that in these first few moments. If they remain silent, then their allegiance to you is infinite and you will be endorsed as their lord.'

'I thought the underworld was dying?' Q said to Hestia. 'How can there be so many creatures still living here if it is a dying world?'

'This is nothing compared to how many there used to be,' Hestia said.

Zam looked on with a mix of wonder and dismay running through him as more and more underworld creatures appeared. He couldn't count how many were present, but their number must have been in the hundreds of thousands and they didn't stop coming until the leaves stopped falling from the sky. Once the last leaf touched the ground, everything fell silent. And everyone looked at Zam.

'I don't know what to say,' Zam said, 'other than I do not think I should be your leader.'

No one responded

'I am only 15 years old.'

'You killed Isaac Bonnyman,' a freaky looking man-giant with the head of a horseshoe bat said.

'And Mandrake Ackx,' a wraith said, 'you defeated him too.'

'What do you want from me?' Zam said.

The mass surrounding Zam parted and he saw a familiar figure walk towards him.

'Your age does not concern me,' Pan said. 'And I do not want anything from you.'

'You are a god; you should be the lord or leader or whatever it is that I don't want to be.'

'I cannot be the lord here.'

'Why not?'

'Because the underworld chose you not me.'

'It made a mistake.'

'That is possible and if it is true, then the underworld will have to live with its mistake, as will the rest of us. There is only one thing that can change things.'

'What?'

'You, Napoleon Xylophone. You can change things.'

'How do I that?'

'By leading in the right way.'

'What is the right way?'

'Lead from the heart when you are unsure and from the head when you know the right thing to do.'

Zam wanted to close his eyes, to make everything go away. He stared at the mass of creatures before him and shook his head. He turned towards Hestia searching for help and saw that she looked unnaturally still, like a TV program that had been paused. Her hand suddenly felt cold. Looking around, he saw that all of the creatures surrounding him; even those in the air, looked exactly the same, like the whole of the Pict underworld had been petrified.

'*You remain unchallenged,*' a female voice sounded all around.

224

Zam tensed when he heard the voice. 'Who are you?' he asked.

'You know who I am.'

The voice was right. Zam knew he was speaking to the Underworld; he just wanted the Underworld to confirm it was true. 'I can't see you, where are you?'

'You can see me. I am the soil beneath your feet, the sky above your head and the air that you breathe.'

'Why have you frozen everything?'

'I wanted to talk to you without distraction.'

'Talk about what?'

'I wanted to welcome you – Patriarch of the Underworld.'

'Patriarch? I thought I was some kind of lord.'

'You are much more than a lord.'

'I don't want to be a lord or a patriarch, whatever that means. I do not want to lead your people.'

'I know.'

'So why do you insist on making me a leader?'

'You are different.'

'I'm not supernatural you mean?'

'There is something about you that I have not felt in any other. You who have talked to Time and who spirits are drawn towards. You are a medium for change.'

'What do you want from me?'

'I want nothing from you other than for you to be yourself.'

'You mean I don't have to stay here? I can go back to Newcastle?'

'Yes, if that is what you choose.'

'How can I be the patriarch if I don't even live here?'

'*The same as you can be Napoleon Xylophone no matter where you live.*'

Zam thought for a while before asking the next question. 'Does the patriarch have any special powers? Can I freeze everyone like you have just now?'

'*You can ask me to do it when you are in the underworld, but you can't harm anything or anyone who is suspended this way. In normal circumstances things are different. You can summon creatures to fight for you, change the weather or the landscape and turn day into night. You can even ask me to destroy the underworld if you so wish.*'

'Why would I want to destroy the underworld?'

'*I do not know. Only you can answer that if the time ever comes when you would want it destroyed.*'

'How do I do all of those things?'

'*Through me.*'

'What, I just say, "Underworld, send a werebeast to fight for me"?'

'*You don't have to say the words. You simply have to think them.*'

Zam thought about rain. It didn't rain. 'I am thinking about rain now, why isn't it pouring down?'

'*You have to think about me making rain.*'

Zam thought about the voice inside his head making rain.

It started to rain.

'Cool!' Zam said out loud, turning his face up to the rainfall. 'You could have helped Bonnyman more in the fight. Why did you allow him to be defeated by Xara and the butcher ghost?'

'I did only what he asked. I cannot do anything more. He did not ask for the right things, so he was defeated.'

'If he had asked for all of his enemies to be covered in lava, would you have done that?'

'Yes, but there is much uncertainty in a request like that – yielding energy that way could have resulted in everyone being covered in lava, including Isaac. You have to be careful what you ask of me.'

Zam stared at the rain falling. It didn't seem to be touching his friends. He remembered what the underworld had said about not being able to harm anyone when everything was suspended.

'Stop raining,' he said inside his mind, directing the command to the Underworld.

It stopped raining.

'Make clouds of vermillion fire burn in the sky. Not too hot that it is uncomfortable.' Zam stared upwards as the underworld sky burned with vermillion clouds of wild fire.

'Unfreeze my friends and the others.'

Zam's friends and the creatures of the underworld slowly began to awaken from their suspended state, seemingly unaware that they had been in any form of suspension. At first staring up at the sky, they soon turned their attention back towards Zam, waiting for him to speak.

'I'm sure you have made a mistake choosing me as your patriarch,' Zam eventually said.

'Patriarch…' Hestia said.

'Yes, the Underworld said I was Patriarch, not Lord.'

There was complete silence in the underworld for a moment as Zam's words sunk in.

'What is it? Zam said.

'If the Underworld has named you Patriarch,' Hestia said, 'then you are not just the leader of the Pict underworld – you are the overlord of every realm in the underworld.'

'Is that true?' Zam said to the Underworld.

'Yes.'

As the sky continued to burn, the creatures of the underworld turned away from Zam and began to fade as they walked off into the distance like shadows vanishing in the mist.

'Where are they going?' Zam asked Hestia.

'To spread the word,' Hestia replied. 'The underworld has a Patriarch for the first time in its history.'

'What does that mean?'

'I do not know, Napoleon. I really do not know.'

When the last of the underworld creatures disappeared, Zam knew in his heart and in his head exactly what he had to do next and, turning from his friends, he made his way to Bonnyman's tent.

25

'What now?' Xara asked Zam.

They were inside Bonnyman's tent and Zam thought she looked more pale than usual, even for a ghost. He didn't want to think how it must have affected her killing Bonnyman, the wraith and seeing her parents murdered. Being killed herself. He didn't want to think about how he was responsible.

'There's something I have wanted to do since we first met Bonnyman,' Zam said.

Wheeling Q up to the crate at the far side of the tent, he lifted the lid and gazed inside. Three kruings, much smaller than the ones Zam had seen Bonnyman eating before sat unassumingly at the bottom of the crate. Zam bent inside and carefully lifted each of the kriungs out. He placed one of the kriungs on Q's left arm rest, one on his right and the third on his lap.

'They are tiny,' Freya said. 'And so cute.'

'What are you going to do with them?' Xara asked.

'I'm going to set them free.'

'That would be a mistake,' Hestia said.

'Why?' Zam asked.

'They were never meant to be free. They do not know how to look after themselves. The first night gaunt they came across would eat them.'

Zam sighed. 'I'm going to keep them, then. I'm going to look after them.'

'Napoleon, I know you mean well,' Hestia said, 'but these creatures do not have a long life span. They only live for a week or two at the most. You have to remember they were created as a source of food.'

'What if I fed them, maybe they would live longer?'

Zam wheeled Q over to the fire and picked up some of the fruit left there. He offered it to the kriungs, but they were uninterested in the food. They never moved at all, never even blinked. It was like they were in an underworld state of perpetual suspension. Zam bent down and picked up a flask of water. He poured some water into the palm of his hand and offered it to each kriung in turn. The kriungs remained unmoved.

'I'm not going to just leave them here,' Zam said, staring at Hestia. 'I'm not going to keep them locked away in that chest until they die.'

'You should name them,' Freya said.

Zam smiled. 'That's a great idea.'

Freya moved to Zam's side and started to stroke one of the kriungs. 'What should we call them?' she said.

'I have no idea,' Zam said.

Freya thought for a moment. 'Maybe you should call them something that's important to you?'

'Yes, but what?'

'That thing you keep saying over and over in your head when you are anxious.'

'What thing?'

'You know, *Xyz*.'

Xara stared at Freya like she had just said something totally shocking.

'How did you know about that?' Zam said.

'I sometimes hear you thinking about it. Even when you are not anxious, it's on your mind.'

'What else do you hear me think about?'

'Nothing else, just *Xyz*. It is obviously very important to you.'

Zam looked embarrassed. 'The first thing I said when I was younger was *Xyz*. I don't know its significance. No one seems to know.'

'Why don't you call one of the kriungs *X*, one *Y* and one *Z*?'

Zam smiled. Then his face turned serious. Then he smiled again. 'I think that's a great idea.'

Xara turned away from Zam and Freya. She looked annoyed, but Zam didn't know what she had to be annoyed about. Maybe she was thinking about her parents.

'Napoleon...' Hestia said.

'Hestia, I don't want to hear any more about it. I'm keeping the kriungs.'

'It's not that, it's your grandfather. He needs us.'

'What?'

'I can sense he is anxious. Something is wrong.'

'I thought everything was over now that we have defeated Bonnyman.'

'This did not start with Isaac and it is not going to end with his death. He did not send the doppelganger or the wraith after you.'

Zam thought back to his conversation with Krackle. 'I'm sure the doppelganger was working with the Cult of the Clan.'

'I'm sure you are right,' Hestia said. 'I just can't see why they want you.'

'Maybe we will find out soon. Do you know where Grandfather is?' Zam said.

'He is still in Edinburgh, at the house.'

'I'm sorry, but we can't go with you,' Eufame said.

Zam could see that Eufame was upset. 'I know,' he said. 'I don't expect you to leave the underworld.'

'It's not the underworld. It's the light,' Eufame said. 'I can feel it searching for me and Freya.'

'That's great,' Zam said, wondering if it was searching for Xara too. Wondering why he hoped it was not.

'We need to hurry,' Hestia said.

'Go now,' Eufame said. 'You do not need to worry about us.'

Zam wasn't worried about them; he knew they were both going to be fine. He was worried about Xara. Why hadn't the light come searching for her? He looked across at her and saw that she was staring into space, her mind on something Zam didn't want to think about.

'Napoleon,' Hestia said. 'We need to leave, now!'

Zam quickly said goodbye to Eufame and Freya and along with Hestia, Xara, the butcher ghost and the three kriungs, they made their way back to the ghost door leading to the City of the Dead. Zam could not explain why he did not sense any real danger threatened his grandfather. What he did sense was that they were walking into a trap – a trap that involved the Cult of the Clan. He was untroubled by this thought though, as now that he could call upon on army to fight alongside him. An underworld army full of wild beasts that would not hesitate if he commanded them to rip apart any Cult of the Clan members who threatened his friends or family.

26

Despite leaving the underworld in daylight, it was night time in Edinburgh when they exited the shop above the City of the Dead. The shop doors were locked, yet even in Q's mangled state he was still able to utilise his lock pick and spring all of the locks they encountered. Once outside, they hailed a taxi and were at the entrance to the house they were staying only a short ride later. The house was dark and silent inside when Zam entered with Hestia at his side. He pressed the light switch, but there was no response.

'Looks like someone has cut the electricity,' Zam said. 'Are any of your lights working Q?'

An LED sprang crookedly from Q's armrest and momentarily flickered into life, before extinguishing almost straight away.

'The light is not cut,' a voice at the other end of the hallway said, 'it is merely distracted.'

As the voice spoke, three vague forms became visible

in front of them. All Zam could make out were their pale faces and black eyes. He saw enough to recognise them as the monsters who took away his mother.

'Where is Eli?' Hestia said.

'And where is my mother?' Zam demanded.

The three figures did not respond at first, instead, they stared at Hestia. 'The old man is safe,' the face to the left said.

'We don't know about the mother,' the face in the middle said.

'You need to come with us,' the face at the end said. 'If you do not, you will leave us no alternative but to harm the old man in a grotesque manner.'

'Napoleon is going nowhere,' Hestia said.

As she spoke, a dim light appeared on the stairway and Zam saw his grandfather standing beside Jha Round. Behind them stood what Zam thought to be a man, but he wasn't sure because the figure's head was covered with bandages. Only his eyes and mouth were uncovered.

'It has never been about the boy,' the bandaged man said. 'It has always been about you, changeling. The boy was simply a lure. A lure to get you out of the Angle underworld. You are far too strong to handle in your own territory.'

'Grandfather, Jha, come down here,' Zam said.

'That wouldn't be a good idea,' the bandaged man said and, as he spoke, the three figures moved to block Eli's path.

'What do you want?' Hestia said.

'Isn't it obvious? We want you. We have always wanted you, the last remaining underworld changeling.'

'There are no other changelings left but me?' Hestia asked.

'Correct,' the bandaged man said.

'Get out of this house,' Zam said, 'before I call upon the underworld creatures to tear you and your pale faced friends apart.'

'How amazing,' the bandaged man said. 'I see you must have killed Isaac. You actually killed him and became lord of his underworld realm.' He slowly clapped his hands. 'Bravo young Xylophone. I thought your victory over Mandrake Ackx was a fluke. Now I see there is more to you than I would ever have guessed.'

'I guess you know all about the creatures I can call upon to fight at my side then.'

'Oh, I do young Xylophone. I also know that you do not understand underworld lore. Tell him about underworld lore, changeling.'

'Tell me what?'

'You are not in the underworld, Napoleon,' Hestia said. 'You cannot call underworld creatures into this world.'

'Why not?'

'You cannot talk to the Underworld here. She cannot hear you.'

'You too, changeling,' the bandaged man said. 'You cannot call upon your underworld creatures either.'

'*Can you hear me?*' Zam said inside his head to the Underworld.

There was a brief moment of silence and Zam thought they must have been right about the Underworld not being able to communicate with him.

He was wrong.

'*Yes, I can hear you.*'

Zam wanted to smile, he didn't though – his face remained pensive. '*They said I couldn't talk to you here. They were lying, right?*'

'*No, they were not lying. You should not be able to talk to me. This has never been possible before.*'

'Either you come with us of your own free will, or we kill your husband and take you by force,' the man said to Hestia.

Eli stared wretchedly at Zam. He looked much older than Zam thought he had ever looked before. Even when he was almost dead in Mandrake Ackx's underworld flames, he had not looked so worn out.

'It's okay, Grandfather,' Zam said. 'I know everything.' He turned towards Hestia. 'Grandmother told me.'

'How sweet,' the bandaged man said, and Zam hated him for saying it the way he did.

'*Can I call upon the creatures of the underworld?*' Zam asked.

'*No, I don't think you can,*' the Underworld answered.

Zam didn't know what the three creatures standing in front of him were, but he didn't think they would easily be beaten in a fight. And what did he have to fight with anyway? He didn't know which, if any, of Q's weapons were still operational. He didn't know if Hestia alone could defeat the three creatures and he wasn't sure if the butcher ghost or Xara would be any use against them either.

'If I come with you, will you leave my family alone?' Hestia asked.

'You have my word,' the bandaged man replied.

'She is not leaving with you,' Zam said. 'I will not allow you to eat her alive.'

'Eat her alive?' Eli said.

'Yes, these are Cult of the Clan. They think eating live changeling flesh will make them immortal.' Zam stared at the bandaged man as he spoke and a thought suddenly came into his head.

'*Can you talk to the butcher ghost?*' he asked the Underworld.

'*Yes.*'

'*Ask him to stand behind the bandaged man. Ask him to do it so the man does not know he is there.*'

'That's absurd,' Eli said. 'Hestia, is it true?'

'Yes. It seems the Clan have been hunting down my kind for the purpose of seeking immortality.' Hestia said.

Zam was pleased when he saw the butcher ghost appear on the steps behind the bandaged man. It was time to see if his hastily formed plan would work.

'You are not immortal yet, are you?' Zam said to the bandaged man.

The man stared at Zam, but did not answer his question.

'Where is Merek? Is he the only one you have successfully made immortal?'

The man still did not respond.

'If you want to become immortal, then you must fear death. Is that right, do you fear death?'

Zam did not wait this time to see if the bandaged man would answer. 'There is a way to prove you do not fear death. If you turn around you will see the ghost who killed Isaac Bonnyman. Isaac was immortal, in a dead kind of way. He died twice. The second time is the last time he will ever die. If you do not leave this house, you will lose your head just like Isaac lost his head.'

The bandaged man did not turn around, instead, he continued to stare at Zam. 'In the time it takes your assassin to kill me, your grandfather and his friend will be killed by my assassins. Then they will kill you. Afterwards, they will overpower your changeling grandmother and take her anyway.'

'I have an alternative to all this death,' Hestia said. 'How much of my flesh do you need right now?'

Zam was sure that the man was smiling behind the bandages. 'Just a sliver,' he said. 'Cut from your arm, perhaps.'

'Hestia, no...' Eli said.

'And if I allow you to cut a sliver from my arm, you will leave and never trouble my family again?' Hestia said.

'In the interest of avoiding unnecessary bloodshed, a sliver of your flesh is a good trade off, for now. I cannot speak for the others though, and say they will never trouble you again.'

Hestia walked over to the edge of the stairs and lifted her sleeve. 'In the interest of time,' she said, 'hurry up and eat.'

The bandaged man slowly pushed past Eli and Jha, making his way towards Hestia.

'Zam, this is wrong,' Xara said. 'You have to stop it.'

'You must not interfere,' the Underworld said. *'For now, there is no other way.'*

As the bandaged man approached Hestia, he drew a dagger from his coat and grabbed hold of Hestia's arm. 'You are very brave, dear,' he said. 'Sacrificing yourself this way.'

'Just get it over with,' Hestia said.

The bandaged man pressed the dagger against Hestia's flesh and began to slice it away from her lower arm. When he had finished, he held a thin strip of her flesh in his hand. Arching back his head, he opened his mouth and dropped Hestia's flesh into it. He chewed on it for a short while before swallowing it. When he was finished, he started to remove the bandage covering his head.

Zam watched the man until the bandage was fully removed and saw that he was a zombie, one that looked ancient compared to Isaac Bonnyman.

'I would not be alive if it was not for the Clan,' he said to Zam. 'I owe them everything.'

The man suddenly bent over double and yelled out in pain. 'It is working,' he said. 'I can feel it working inside me.' He pressed his hands to his face. 'I can feel it working here too.'

Zam took his eyes away from the man for a moment and stared at Hestia, who was holding her arm where the flesh had been sliced away. Although her arm had healed and no longer bled, there was a hollow where the flesh had been cut away. After seeing her morph into so many different forms, Zam had expected her arm to return to its former shape. He was sad to see that it had not.

The man stood up straight and Zam saw that his face was no longer zombified. He didn't look ancient either; he had the face of an unremarkable man in his early twenties.

'There is one more thing I need to confirm,' the man said, taking the dagger and sinking it into his heart. He gasped in pain, but stood there for a moment, staring directly at Hestia. Then he removed the dagger from his chest, wiped the blood from it on his sleeve and put the dagger inside his coat.

'Go now,' Hestia said to the man.

The man smiled at Hestia. 'Thank you,' he said, before turning to the three creatures and nodding in the direction of the door.

Zam tensed as they neared him and gripped tightly

on Q's armrests. 'What about my mother,' he said to them as they passed by him.

The man did not answer. He exited the house with the three creatures following closely behind. As they disappeared into the night, Zam felt a violent urge to chase after them and hit them with whatever weapons Q had available. Feeling Xara's ghostly hand on his shoulder, he relaxed a little, and hearing her speak, made up his mind not to follow them.

'Your grandmother needs you, Zam,' she said. 'And so do I.'

27

'Is my mother dead?' Zam asked Hestia.

They were in the lounge, sitting on the oversized couches drinking hot coffee that Jha had prepared for them. Xara and the butcher ghost stood side-by-side behind the couches, watching intently.

'I think so,' Hestia replied. 'Even though she was only half changeling, the Clan must have used her in their quest for immortality. The man said I was the last remaining changeling.'

Zam stared at his feet. 'And my father?'

'We haven't heard from him in over a year,' Eli said. 'It is the longest he has ever gone without letting us know where he is or what he is doing.'

'Is there any way of contacting him?' Zam asked.

'We have an email address,' Eli said.

'I want that address. I want to send him an email.'

'Of course,' Eli said.

'And I want you and Grandmother to stay together. It was stupid of you two staying apart because of me.'

'It wasn't stupid,' Xara said. 'They did it for the right reasons. I think it was incredibly romantic.'

Zam was going to say something in response, but changed his mind.

'What do we do about the Clan? Is it over?' Xara asked.

'This isn't finished,' Zam said. 'Krackle was vague when I questioned him, but I got the impression there was more than one man looking for immortality. I got the impression he was working for the Clan because he thought they were going to make everyone in the underworld immortal.'

'Immortality in the here and now is against the will of God,' Hestia said. 'The creatures of the underworld would not look for immortality before they die.'

'Krackle thinks God has abandoned the underworld. Maybe there are others who think the same way.'

'The Clan are amazingly gifted if they have succeeded in convincing underworld creatures about that lie,' Hestia said.

'The man said he would not trouble us again,' Eli said.

'Do you trust him?' Zam asked.

'From the little I know about the Clan, they seem to keep their word. Honour is a precious commodity in any culture,' Hestia said. 'The problem is not the man we encountered tonight, but other Clan members who made no such promise.'

'I don't trust him. I don't trust the Clan at all,' Zam said.

244

Hestia looked troubled. 'Even if he is not to be trusted, we know we are safe in the underworld.'

'You think we should stay in the underworld and hide from the Clan?'

'Perhaps it would be wise,' Eli said. 'Until we at least know a little more about what just happened.'

'Yes,' Hestia said.

'Those three creatures were the ones who took my mother from me. What are they?' Zam asked Hestia.

'They are Morbanes,' Hestia said. 'Neither creatures of this world or the underworld – they are demons contracted from hell.'

'What do you mean, contracted?'

'The only way to get a demon working for you is to draw up a contract with them. Once the contract is signed, they will do your bidding until the terms of the contract are met. I hate to think what price the Clan had to pay for the services of not one, but three Morbanes.'

'How can I kill them?'

'Napoleon...' Eli started.

'They killed my mother,' Zam said.

'It is not that you can kill them, it is more that you cast them back to hell.'

'How do I do that?'

'You don't, only a necromancer has the knowledge and power to fight demons.'

'Where do I find a necromancer?'

Eli sighed heavily. 'Your father is a necromancer,' he said.

'It's been a long day,' Hestia said. 'You need to sleep Napoleon.'

'Your...grandmother is right,' Eli said. 'I need to sleep too, I'm exhausted. We can talk again tomorrow with clearer heads.'

'Fine,' Zam said. 'I need more answers tomorrow though, especially about my father.' He turned towards Jha who was sitting next to Q, surveying the damage he sustained when he fell from the sky. 'How does he look, Jha?'

Jha bit on the screwdriver he was holding. 'Not good, we may have to start from scratch again.'

'You are going to give me a new body, just when I was getting used to this one,' Q said.

'I was thinking with your next body, we could make it so that you can transform into a motorbike – something like a Norton Commander. What do you think?'

'When can you start?' Q said.

Zam stood up from the couch and sat in Q. 'We need to fix him as soon as possible.'

Jha nodded his head in agreement. 'We will have to get him back to the workshop in Newcastle.'

'Can't you fix him in the underworld?' Hestia said.

'We could, but it would take longer,' Eli answered.

'I don't think I like the sound of the underworld,' Jha said.

'You will learn to love it, Jha, worry not,' Eli said.

Zam said goodnight to everyone and wheeled himself to his bedroom. At the door he turned around and looked at Xara and the butcher ghost who had followed him. 'I don't think it would be a good idea for all of us to sleep in the same room tonight.'

'I don't want to be left on my own tonight,' Xara said. 'Please let me stay with you.'

Zam stared at the butcher ghost, ready to say something, but before he could, the ghost vanished.

'Is he just invisible or has he left us?' Zam asked Xara.

'I can't feel his presence, I think he has gone to wherever it is he disappears to from time to time.'

'I'm sorry for everything that's happened to you.'

'Don't be dumb. It's not your fault.'

'Are you okay?'

'Of course I'm not okay.'

'Is there anything I can do to help?'

'Yes, hurry up and get in your bedroom and go to sleep.'

'What do you do while I'm sleeping?'

'She stares at you most of the night, Zam,' Q said.

'I practice ghostly things,' Xara quickly said.

'What kind of ghostly things?' Zam asked.

'How to move things with my mind. How to become invisible. How to read your dreams. Sometimes I even join you in your dreams. You can't see me, but I am close by. Maybe one day, with practice, you will see me like I see you in your dreams.'

Zam sighed and entered the bedroom. He got the kriungs out of the rucksack and sat them on top of the bed. He stared into their eyes but saw no signs of awareness. Feeling exhausted, he lay down on top of the bed and fell asleep almost immediately.

28

'I know where I'm buried,' Xara said. 'Will you come to my grave with me?'

It was early the next morning. They were in Zam's bedroom. He was stroking the three kriungs X, Y, and Z.

All three of them had died in the night.

'Yes, of course I will.'

'I'm sorry about your kriungs.'

Zam stopped stroking the kriungs and gently placed them on the bedside cabinet. He pulled the blankets off his legs. He lay down on his back and started his leg stretches.

'I thought they were the reason *Xyz* was so important to me.' Zam said. 'I thought I could keep them alive.'

'I know,' Xara said. 'I'm sorry.' She got off the chair and walked over to Zam where she held her hands under his legs to support them while he stretched.

'Would you mind if I buried them next to you?' Zam said.

'No, that would be fine.'

'I'll leave a note for Grandfather and... Grandmother. So they know where we are going.'

'I had my first dream last night.'

Zam turned towards Xara and smiled. 'What did you dream about?'

'I dreamt about being in space.'

'Like an astronaut?'

'No, I wasn't wearing a space suit; I was dressed like this, staring at a ringed planet. I think I was on a moon.'

'It sounds like you were dreaming about Titan, a moon that orbits Saturn. It rains methane drops in slow motion there.'

'It was raining in my dream, but not methane drops.'

'What then?'

'It was raining leaves, like it was in the underworld.'

'That's some dream. I wish I was there.'

'You were there. You were acting strange, like you were lost or something.'

'That's probably because I was in your dream and not my own.

They both laughed.

Zam stopped stretching his legs.

'It's time I washed,' he said.

'Yes,' Xara said.

'Thanks for telling me about your dream. I like the idea of it raining leaves on Titan.'

'Me too.'

'I don't want any light taking you away.' Zam said,

swinging his legs over the side of the bed before making his way to the bathroom.

Xara smiled as Zam closed the door behind him.

***

Zam rang for a taxi after he washed. He was pleased Xara did not speak during the journey. Not just because it would have made the taxi driver think Zam was talking to himself, but also because the lack of distraction gave him time to think about everything that had happened since Krackle first introduced himself in the bathroom mirror. Xara sat in the seat next to him, and Zam could hardly imagine what it must feel like to visit her own grave, thinking about the body she had been connected to buried in the earth beneath her.

Too weird.

The taxi pulled into the road across from the cemetery and the driver got out. He lifted Q from the boot and positioned him near to the passenger door while Zam shuffled off the taxi seat and sat in Q.

'Someone special waiting for you in there?' the taxi driver asked.

'Yes, someone very special,' Zam said as he paid the driver.

Xara bit her lip, staring at the floor. Zam couldn't tell if she was pleased at what he said.

After the driver pulled away, Zam followed Xara up

the path into the cemetery. She walked slowly, seemingly reluctant to arrive at her graveside. She stopped next to a plain headstone and Zam watched as she stared down at the earth. Two freshly dug graves were situated next to Xara's and Zam realised she had been buried alongside her parents.

Zam read Xara's headstone.

In loving memory of Xara Yvette Zook
Cherished and greatly missed by her family

Zam read the headstone again barely able to comprehend what he was reading.

'Xara, your full name...' He said.

Xara continued to look down at her grave as she spoke. 'Yes.'

'You are Xyz.'

'I think so. I think I've known it for a while.'

'Why didn't you say anything?'

'I don't know, I guess I was scared.'

'Scared of what?'

'That you'd be disappointed once you discovered who I was.'

'Are you crazy, why would I be disappointed?'

'I'm just a ghost, that's all, Zam, a ghost.'

Zam stared at Xara for a moment then pulled the rucksack from the back of Q. The kriungs were inside. 'We should bury these now,' he said.

'Yes,' Xara said.

Zam unbuckled himself from Q and walked as best he could over to Xara's grave. He sat down next to her and pulled a trowel out of the rucksack that he had put there before they left the house. He started to dig and Xara sat down beside him, watching. When he had removed enough soil, he gently pulled out the kriungs one at a time and placed them in the hole he had just dug. Once all three were in the hole, he covered them with soil.

'I don't know what to say,' Zam said, once he had finished burying the kriungs.

Xara sighed. 'Me either.'

'Xyz,' Zam said.

'Yes.'

'I love your name, Xara Yvette Zook.'

'Thank you.'

'We should get back. They will be worried.'

Zam stood up and got back into Q.

'Will you hold my hand?' Xara said.

'Yes,' Zam said, taking hold of her hand as they made their way out of the cemetery. At the gate he repeated his mantra inside his head, even though he did not feel anxious or threatened. '*Xara Yvette Zook*,' he said over and over again.

Author Note

Taken from Napoleon Xylophone, the first part of the trilogy:

Napoleon Xylophone sprung to life from two independent sources. The first source came during a lecture as part of an MA in creative writing I undertook at Teesside University. During the lecture I was asked to develop a writing workshop directed at a group or organization where I had an interest or affiliation. The second and most important source came from my eleven year-old son, Michael and the ambassador club he attended with Whizz-Kidz, a UK based charity working with disabled children. Michael has a walking disability which means he has to spend most of his time in a wheelchair. We often talked about the lack of disabled superheroes in fiction novels or in movies and I saw this workshop as an opportunity to create a superhero for Michael and other disabled children. After discussing the idea with Whizz-kidz they gave the go-ahead for me to run five workshops with their children based at Newcastle.

As well as creating a different kind of superhero

another aim of the project was to give disabled children a different kind of voice, one which allowed them to express how they fit into society without coming across as crusaders looking for sympathy. This new voice was spoken through a fifteen year-old schoolboy called Napoleon Xylophone. Right at the start it was agreed that our superhero would not have special powers like Superman. Our hero needed to use his wits and gadgets like Batman to help get himself out of trouble. As he travelled through the pages of his story Napoleon shows the difficulties disabled children encounter in everyday life. Issues such as people staring, bullying, difficulties getting into shops, onto public transport or simply crossing the road were all discussed by the children.

During the workshops we also looked at characterization and plot, with the children putting forward suggestions for story development as well as character names. Mandrake Ackx was one of the names they suggested, along with supernatural creatures such as changelings and ghosts with bad memories.

After completing the workshop and coming up with some great ideas, it seemed a shame to leave Napoleon unpublished. No mainstream publisher was going to publish a book like Napoleon Xylophone and after failing to obtain support from the Arts Council, we decided to publish his story ourselves. That was when the second part of Napoleon's adventure started with fundraising activities that included a sponsored walk along an eighteen mile stretch of water by the banks of the river Tees. The journey took the participants from Bowes Museum at Barnard Castle to Broken Scar near Darlington town centre. Funds raised from the walk along with a contribution from a local firm meant we had enough money to self-publish Zam's story. I hope you enjoyed his story and perhaps got a small insight into what life is like in a wheelchair.

After completing Xyz:

When my son was younger he placed a small note on my pillow for me to see at bedtime. On the upturned side his young hand had written – I am the Macaracoon warrior.It made me smile. As I picked up the note, I noticed there was something else written on the other side. Checking it out I saw that he had written in bold handwriting – **I don't want to be disabled!**

Reading his words made me want to do everything in my power to make him not feel that way.

Napoleon Xylophone is for the Macaracoon warrior and anyone else looking for a different kind of hero.

Acknowledgements

David Simpson and Richard Thomas for two great reviews and invaluable feedback.

Mizz Middle for all those proof reads and words of encouragement.

Anton Semenov – what an illustrator!

Everyone at Matador for the great looking books they have produced, as well as their marketing efforts and support.

My son, Mikey, without him Napoleon Xylophone and Witching Hole simply would not exist.

If you want to find out more about the author, you can check him out here:

franklambert.co.uk